IVAI

Th

Ken could never have known what would happen when he left Melbourne to stay with Uncle Bob's family in the hills for the whole holiday weekend. Nothing turned out as he'd planned, though he'd been looking forward to the visit – his first real trip on his own – for months and months. But when the boys camp out and Ken, chasing a marauding fox, finds himself trapped in an old gold-mining shaft with a sinister history, events rise to an almost unbearable pitch of tension and excitement. And neither Ken, nor Hugh and Joan and Francie, nor their parents, are ever the same again . . .

IVAN SOUTHALL

THE FOX HOLE

Illustrated by Ian Ribbons

MAMMOTH

First published in Great Britain 1967
by Methuen Co Ltd and
published simultaneously in Australia
by Hicks, Smith & Sons Pty Ltd
Magnet paperback edition published 1980
Reprinted 1985
Published 1989 by Mammoth
an imprint of Mandarin Paperbacks
Michelin House, 81 Fulham Road, London SW3 6RB

Mandarin is an imprint of the Octopus Publishing Group

Text copyright © 1967 Ivan Southall
Illustrations copyright © 1967 Methuen & Co Ltd
Cover artwork copyright © 1980 Methuen Children's
Books Ltd

ISBN 0 7497 0363 6

A CIP catalogue record for this title is available
from the British Library

Printed in Great Britain
by Cox & Wyman Ltd., Reading

To Michele

CONTENTS

Place names in this story are real; perhaps, in a way, some of the people are, too, though I would be very surprised if any of them came to your house for tea. Something happens to them, of course, or there wouldn't be a story to tell, and even that has a bit of truth in it. But don't go looking for the Fox Hole. Take my word for it, it's much, much better to keep away.

Chapter One

THE NIGHT KEN CAME

When he thought about it afterwards, with that funny little shiver that came with the remembering of it, Hugh was not sure how it had started.

In fact, Hugh had never thought seriously about anything much before. He was the sort of boy who just did things – good or bad – because they were there to be done. If he wanted to chop down a tree, he chopped it down whether he was supposed to or not. If he wanted to talk in class he talked. If he wanted to get up at four o'clock in the morning he got up. If he wanted a fight, as he often did, he picked one with the nearest person handy. (For the same reason he boasted to Charlie Baird, 'Scared? Me? I bet you I will sleep down in the gully.') Hugh, as far as his parents were concerned, was a stocky, snub-nosed lump of trouble. He wouldn't *think*. 'Think! Think! Think!' his father used to screech at him.

But this time it was different. This time it was not just Hugh breaking a window or Hugh falling

out of a tree or Hugh putting worms in his sisters'
beds; this time everyone was involved – the whole
family – Hugh, Joan, Francie, Mum, Dad, and
Ken, too.

It had happened, and there had been amazement
and excitement and trouble. The grown-ups had
started acting strangely. Mum and Dad had been
difficult. Dad had been wide-eyed at first, stunned
almost, then had laughed like someone a bit silly in
the head, but in a while he had become tense and
irritable, sometimes looking at Mum in an odd sort
of way and Mum had giggled nervously like a
girl.

There seemed to be so many points at which it
could have started. It could have been Ken; the
night Ken came. (There was no doubt about that,
really.) Poor Ken. It could have been the fox. Or all
four might have started it, with other things
added.

In a way it seemed that the trouble had been
there all the time, like a date on the calendar, just
waiting to happen. For years and years, just waiting to happen. For fifty years, sixty years, seventy
years, perhaps eighty years lying there in wait, like
a huge boulder at the brink of a high cliff waiting to
fall, or an uninvited visitor knock-knock-knocking
at the door, waiting to get in. For years children
had known that something was wrong in the gully.
For eighty years, waiting.

'How long is eighty years, Dad?'

'A long time, Hugh.'

'Yeh. But how long?'

'I don't know, son. You'd have to ask someone much older than I am.'

Hugh thought that over. He believed he knew what his father meant. Someone had to live for eighty years to know really how long it was. 'How old are you, Dad?'

Dad smiled and made everything right with the world again. Dad hadn't smiled in that particular way for days. While it had lasted he had been a very strange man indeed, and for days afterwards, stranger still. But by the time that Hugh had started really thinking about it the trouble had gone away and Ken had gone away too.

The night Ken came was the Friday of the holiday long weekend, and people with suitcases and haversacks were on the Hills' train, all mixed up with business men and secretaries and shop assistants going home for tea.

It was all very new for Ken, that hot, crowded and noisy train. Grown-ups, tired after a day's work, reading newspapers or books or magazines, or nodding as though about to drop off to sleep, late shoppers getting home from the city all smothered in parcels, rowdy groups of young people dressed for roughing it in the bush, troops of Boy Scouts singing camp-fire songs – and Ken: Ken, so very quiet and for the time being nervous in the middle of it, in that swaying, noisy train, the 5.10 from Melbourne on the eve of the holiday long week-end.

Ken sat at the edge of the seat on a few spare inches between two very big men, clutching his heavy suitcase because there was not any room left for it on the luggage-rack, aching because he was so uncomfortable, sweating because he was so hot, his eyes smarting from tobacco smoke.

He was excited, of course he was, but he had never been in a train before on his own, never gone anywhere on his own before, except to school or to the local shops for Mum or for play or sport or something like that close to home. For a long time, as this weekend had come nearer, he had somehow imagined that the carriage would be empty except for himself. He would sit at the window counting stations and level-crossings, looking out for cows and horses, listening to the clickety-clack of the train rushing him up into the hills where Hugh and Joan lived. But it wasn't like that.

There were so many people and so much noise and he could hardly see anything at all, just glimpses past newspapers and broad backs. People did get out at times, but more crowded in. He was pushed and pummelled by legs and elbows and swinging haversacks. His feet were trodden on. His flushed face was clipped by the edges of suitcases. His hair was ruffled by parcels and sleeves. And he ached and ached because his own suitcase was so heavy. It was quite the longest hour of his whole life.

At Belgrave, the end of the line, people poured out of the train as though swept along by a river and Ken was carried forward with them, almost ready to cry. He had never imagined anything like it. It was such a struggle to stay on his feet, to lug that suitcase, to be hemmed in and carried forward by a bustling forest of people as tall as trees, up that long, steep ramp, not really knowing where he was going, except that he hoped to find the bus at the end of it.

His mother had told him where the bus would be, but he couldn't think, he couldn't remember, and though he called in a plaintive voice, 'Where do I get the bus for Monbulk?' no one seemed to hear. They were all hurrying for their own buses, all those big, busy people. They didn't care whether a little boy was lost or frightened or trampled underfoot. And Ken felt very little. He had never felt littler, ever.

'Monbulk you want, do you?' a voice said.

It was a man, bending down, walking, hurrying beside him, a vague sort of big man.

'Oh, yes, please.'

'Come along then.'

Ken stumbled in pursuit of the big, vague man, afraid he was going to lose sight of him, because dragging that suitcase was like dragging an anchor.

The man looked back. 'Come on, lad.'

Ken must have looked desperate because the man waited.

'What have you got there?' he said. 'Bricks?' Then he took the suitcase from him as though it weighed absolutely nothing and was off again with long strides, Ken almost running to keep up, saying, 'Thank you. Thank you. Thank you very much.'

The man didn't reply, perhaps didn't even hear, just strode along the top of the ramp and down the other side.

'There's your bus,' the man said, 'that one.' And suddenly Ken was on his own again, with his suitcase as heavy as an anchor, with people pressing around him in the queue for a big red bus, and he was so close to crying that he was scared the tears were showing. He had looked forward to the adventure of travelling on his own, to going somewhere by himself instead of in the family car, to paying his own fare like a grown-up, to doing everything right so that his mother would allow him to do it again. It was beaut in the hills with Auntie Kath and Uncle Bob and his cousins. He hadn't wanted a single little thing to spoil a single minute of it.

People were pushing, and he struggled up the high steps dragging the awful suitcase, and the driver was sitting there, red in the face because of the heat, holding out his hand for money.

*   *   *

'Where to?' the driver asked, almost as if he didn't know where his bus was supposed to go.

'Monbulk,' Ken said in alarm. 'You're going there, aren't you? To Monbulk?'

'Ten cents.'

Ken couldn't find the purse his mother had given him.

'Come on, sonny. Ten cents.'

The driver's face seemed to loom closer, to become even redder, to become threatening, but it didn't. Ken only thought so.

'Have you got your fare or haven't you?'

Ken nodded vigorously while he ran his hands frantically from pocket to pocket.

'In you get then,' the driver said. 'Down the back. Pay on the way out. Put your case over there behind the rail. Don't block the aisle with it, sonny. Come on, come on! Take the kid's case, someone. Chuck it in there.'

Ken sobbed, but no one heard him. Everyone was too hot to listen or too anxious to get home or too busy scrambling for seats. It was nearly half past six; the last bus of the day. It was terrible the way people pushed each other.

Ken stumbled to the back of the bus but there were no seats left and he had to stand while he hunted through his pockets for his purse, feeling sick, feeling weak, shaking. It wasn't there. And it had the return half of his train ticket in it and twenty cents for bus fares and fifty cents to spend.

He searched for a kind face, for someone like the
nice, vague man, but people were just too hot or
tired or too busy thinking their own thoughts to
worry about an unhappy ten-year-old who didn't
know whether to cry or run back to the train, to
pound up and down the ramps shouting, 'My purse,
I've lost my purse. It's gone.' But no one seemed to
be looking his way. They were looking at newspapers again, or magazines or books, or out through
the windows or talking to each other. Inside Ken
there seemed to be a great big hole, a great big
blackness, a great big fright. Then it was too late to
do anything because the bus started and he had to
hang on or be jerked from his feet.

'I've lost my purse,' he whimpered to himself,
'and Auntie Kath and Uncle Bob can't give me any
more. They haven't got any money. Mum's always
saying that they haven't got any money. And it
must be true or she wouldn't have put all those tins
of things in my suitcase and made it so heavy.'

The bus turned this way and that, crabbing
round corners and curves like a long, stiff animal
that was sore in the joints, and Ken swayed with it,
feeling sick. It climbed into the great green forest
where trees were towers and met with arching
boughs high above the road. It was like the nave of
a cathedral with bends in it, like a cathedral that
had come alive and was twisting slowly through
shafts of sunlight, like a cathedral full of worship-
pers with wheels on.

Slow traffic, throaty with sound; cars with cara-
vans behind them laboriously climbing, other cars
as busy as beetles darting in and out trying to break
free, to get out in front, car-loads of young people,
truck-loads of Boy Scouts and campers, thundering
semi-trailers belching oil fumes and stacked high
and swaying with cases of fruit for the jam factory;
Ken swaying, too, holding to the rail on the back of
a seat, despairing.

People called the forest Sherbrooke. Sometimes
when Ken drove through with his family he
thought of Robin Hood. Robin's forest was half the
world away, thousands of miles across the sea, and
had a slightly different name. But only slightly
different. He thought of Robin Hood in Sherwood
robbing the rich to give to the poor, to give to boys
who had lost their purses and to Aunties and Uncles
who didn't have any money.

Then he got thinking about gold. It was the
evening sunlight on the trees and the shafts of sunlight striking the road and the glow of sunlight in
the air. The world had turned to gold. The forest
was made of solid gold. If anyone wanted a bunch
of gold they went into the forest and picked it. If
anyone wanted a log of gold they cut down a tree.
But there was so much gold that it wasn't worth
anything. Everybody had too much of it. Even a
boy couldn't pay a bus fare with it.

Hugh, Joan and Francie waited at the bus stop.

Francie was six and had everything that made grown-ups go all silly: huge green eyes, long golden hair and a face that was so, so beautiful. The other half of the story her brother and sister knew best.

Francie wrote her name on everything: on floors and walls and other people's homework. She cut pictures out of books that didn't belong to her. She talked from half past six in the morning until half past seven at night. If someone was talking up a tree or under the house or inside a cupboard or a hundred yards down the road, it was Francie.

'When's the bus coming?' Francie said eight times. 'Will Ken have a lolly for me?' she said six times. 'I want Ken to sleep in my room,' she said four times. 'I like Ken 'cos he doesn't tell me to shut up like you do, Joan. You're not allowed to say shut up to me. It's rude. I'll tell Mummy you said shut up to me. We've got sweet corn for tea 'cos Ken's coming. I like lots of butter on my sweet corn. Does Ken like lots of butter on his sweet corn?'

Joan was very, very much older than Francie. She was ten and a quarter. She could make her bed and wash the dishes and use the vacuum cleaner and bake a chocolate cake. She was good at history but bad at arithmetic. She had a snub nose like her brother, a cat, three bantams and a collection of different coloured stones. Also twenty-three books and a shelf to put them on.

'I'm sure the bus is late,' she said. 'Do you think

it's had an accident? Wouldn't it be awful? First
time an' all that Ken's come on it. With all this
traffic on the road it might have gone over the edge
or something up past The Patch.'

Hugh said, 'I reckon we ought to go fishing in the
Woori tomorrow. Charlie Baird's been catching
rainbow trout down in the Woori. Wouldn't it be
beaut if we caught a trout? We could take sand-
wiches with us and maybe cook the trout. Do you
reckon we'd be allowed to light a fire?'

Francie said, 'Ken's going to play Tops and Tails
with me. Ken's not going to go home tomorrow, is
he? I'm allowed to stay up till nine o'clock tonight,
Mummy said. When's the bus coming?'

Joan said, 'I hope Ken brings his stamps. I've got
some to swop. I hope he brings his togs and we can
swim in the dam.'

Hugh said, 'I reckon we ought to go to the Bald
Hills on Sunday and look for old gold-mines. After
Sunday School, that is. Do you reckon we'll have to
go to Sunday School? Maybe we can make some
bows and arrows and shoot a rabbit for lunch.
Charlie Baird shot a rabbit with a bow and
arrow.'

Chapter Two

THE SCREECH-OWL

The bus hadn't had an accident; hadn't driven over the edge of the cliff up past The Patch; hadn't even run out of petrol a mile down the road. It arrived and everyone got out except Ken.

'He's not on it,' shrieked Francie. 'Where's Ken?'

'Ken's missed it,' wailed Joan, 'and there's not another bus until tomorrow.'

'Gee,' said Hugh, 'Ken hasn't come.'

'Yes, he has,' shrieked Francie. 'There's Ken. Ken's there. You will sleep in my room, won't you, Ken?'

Ken was there, talking to the driver.

His head was swaying from side to side in an awkward way, he was rubbing his forehead with his hand, and he had a very guilty look as though he had been caught stealing apples or had ripped the seat clean out of his pants.

'I can't find it, I can't, I can't,' he was clearly saying. 'I'm awfully sorry, Mr Driver. I'm terrible sorry, Mr Driver. I wouldn't travel without a fare, Mr Driver, really I wouldn't. I've lost my train ticket home an' everything. It's all gone. I must have dropped it or something. I don't know where it's gone. I'll send the money, Mr Driver, really I will. I promise. I promise. I really will send it.'

And the driver, trying to make himself heard over Ken's outburst was saying, 'All right, sonny; all right, all right! We all lose things; it can't be helped. I'm not going to shoot you. For cryin' out loud, you're not going to get shot! Pay me next time if you must, but get outa here. Please, sonny, *go*!'

So Ken came reeling down to the kerb, dragging his suitcase from step to step: bump, bump, bump; flushed and sniffly, making funny nervous expressions with his mouth and muttering, 'Golly, golly, golly.'

'Ken,' shrieked Francie. 'Hullo, Ken. We've got sweet corn for tea 'cos you're coming.'

'Gee, Ken,' said Hugh, 'what's up?'

'He's lost his *purse*,' cried Joan. 'You heard.'

'Yeh,' sniffed Ken, manfully trying to wish back the tears that were showing. 'Lost me purse just like a little kid.'

'Gee, Ken.'

'All me money and everything. Mum'll skin me. She won't let me come again; I know she won't.'

'Of course she will,' said Joan. 'I'll bet she's lost her purse lots of times. My mum's always losing hers.'

'*Always?*'

'Puts it down and can't find it. Leaves it in shops and things. Grown-ups are always losing their purses, aren't they, Hugh?'

'Yeh,' said Hugh, 'of course they are. Losin' purses is nothin'.'

'We've got sweet corn for tea,' screeched Francie. 'Do you like sweet corn, Ken? I like lots of butter on my sweet corn.'

'We're camping out tonight, Ken,' Hugh said. 'I've put the tent up and all.'

'He's sleeping in my room,' screeched Francie, 'aren't you, Ken?'

Joan said, 'He's camping out with Hugh down at the dam, because Hugh's put the tent up and fixed it with Mum. He had to do some nagging, I'm telling you, what with the gully and all. Hugh's brave. Then I'm cooking the breakfast and taking it down at seven o'clock: rice bubbles and toast and honey and everything. Then we're going to have a swim, aren't we, Ken, when our breakfast's gone down. Dad says we're lucky to have the water because it's been such a dry season.'

But Ken was lost. Most of their words were running over the top of him, not sinking in. He was worried because Auntie Kath was always losing her purse and because Francie liked lots of butter. If they kept on losing purses all the time and kept on eating lots of butter all the time no wonder they didn't have any money. And they didn't seem to care either. Back home in Ken's house it was different.

Then Joan said, 'Come on, or it'll be dark before we get there and Mum'll have a fit. She'll be out the front shoutin' and screaming. We'll hear her a mile away. She hates us being out on the road after dark.'

'Yeh, come on, Ken,' said Hugh. 'Forget the silly old purse. Mum'll give you some money.' Then Hugh picked up the suitcase. 'Gee. It's heavy. By the time we get home it'll weigh a ton. There's nothing you can chuck away, is there?'

Ken almost yelled. 'No! Of course there's not. But you didn't *walk* in, did you? Not two miles? What about the car?'

'Busted again,' said Hugh. 'The fellas at the garage reckon Dad ought to put a bomb in it.'

'To make it go bang-bang,' screeched Francie. 'We're going to have a big bang and everyone's coming to watch. Daddy's going to blow it up. *Bang!*'

'He's going to fix it up for us to play with,' said Joan. 'He's going to fix it up so we can drive it round and round the paddock.'

'So *you* can?' squealed Ken.

'So Hugh can. Hugh's eleven. I'm only ten.'

'Yes,' said Hugh. 'Charlie Baird's father fixed up an old Chev for him to drive round the paddock. He's had three crashes already. It's beaut. Maybe we can have a ride in it tomorrow if Charlie'll let us.'

Ken felt all weak in the legs. 'No . . .'

'Gee. You're not chicken or anythin', are you? You can't get hurt. It only goes ten miles an hour. But the kids can do forty down Seamer's Hill on their bikes. Whooh! You oughta watch 'em go. Mum won't let me any more, because last time I broke my arm and busted me bike . . . Gee, Ken. Shake a leg. Don't stand there like a stunned chook.'

So Ken went with them, in a muddle, already dragging his feet at the thought of those two deadly miles, at the thought of hills where boys on bikes could do forty miles an hour going down. But he'd be going up, not down! And sleeping in a tent next to the dam. In the dark. In that bush full of cats' eyes and snakes' eyes and all sorts of sounds. And swimming in the dam! He'd put his toe in it once and it was like ice. And crashing in cars. And sweet corn; he hated sweet corn.

Nothing was what he had thought it would be, not from the very beginning, not from the moment he had stepped on the train. Even Hugh and Joan were different and Francie was terrible, screeching all the time. And Uncle Bob and Auntie Kath sounded like different people, too; nothing like the sensible people they were when they came visiting or when Ken went to see them with his mother and father. He was even frightened of all the weird things his cousins said.

In Ken's house everything was so very different

from this. Ken's father was an executive in a company that made cardboard boxes; an important job, Mum said. But Uncle Bob didn't do anything at all, just loafed round the house all day. That must have been the difference; it just hadn't shown before.

Mum was always talking about them in a funny sort of way, particularly when Ken said anything nice about Uncle Bob, which wasn't difficult, because Uncle Bob was so very nice – or Ken had thought he was. She was always saying things that had never made sense until now. Things like, 'Your Uncle Bob was never a proper brother to me. He led me a terrible life. He was never any good and never will be. Never done an honest day's work in his life. Writing rhymes for birthday cards! Painting stupid little pictures! All for peanuts. What sort of work is that for a grown man? No wonder his wife's a bundle of nerves. Living in that wretched little house. As hot as an oven in summer; as cold as the grave in winter. Every time it rains the roof leaks. Every time the wind blows it's a wonder it doesn't fall down.'

Then only this morning Mum had said, 'I am letting you go, Kenneth, with the gravest misgivings.' But she'd stopped herself rather awkwardly and changed the subject. Ken wasn't sure what 'gravest misgivings' were, but he had an idea. 'Oh, golly,' he mumbled to himself, 'isn't it awful? And I'm stuck here till Monday night.'

Francie was shrieking in his ear again and Hugh was dragging the suitcase along the gravel road with a horrible scratching sound and Joan was telling them that the sun had set and if they were not to be caught in the dark they would have to hurry.

'Mum'll give us the rounds of the kitchen if we don't get home before dark. She's had a thing about it ever since the screech-owl.'

'Uh?' said Ken.

'It makes a noise at night like someone getting murdered. First time she heard it she rang the police. They were searching the bush for days. She

still reckons it wasn't a bird. She still reckons there's a body in the bush.'

It was not really a wretched little house where Uncle Bob and Auntie Kath lived. It might have leaked a bit when it rained, it might have shaken a bit when the wind blew hard, but it never looked like falling down, particularly not now in the flattering light of dusk. It looked like a palace with all its welcoming windows gleaming through the roadside trees. It looked like the right sort of end to a long walk. Ken could almost hear his mother saying, as she had said before, 'Every light in the place on again – of course!' It wasn't like that at Ken's place; indeed it was not.

'Sweet corn,' screeched Francie, 'goodie, goodie.' And went scuttling down the road, shrieking, 'Ken's come, Mummy. Ken's here. Ken's here. Ken's going to sleep in my room, isn't he?'

No one took any notice of Francie. Francie went on shrieking or chattering and everyone went on ignoring her. She was chattering even on the door-step and through the living-room and in the kitchen while Auntie Kath kissed Ken and Uncle Bob shook his hand. Francie just went on chattering like a wireless in the background, turned up loud, that no one listened to or bothered to switch off. They simply talked over her.

The noise bewildered Ken because he was tired and footsore and miserable deep inside, though he wore a smile and said 'Yes' or 'No' in the right places. He could not understand why he had not noticed before that they made such a dreadful row in the house. Ken's home was quiet and orderly, with hardly ever a raised voice; even arguments were conducted quietly in case the neighbours heard.

There was Hugh blowing on his hands and telling everyone that they were like 'bloomin' lumps of meat' from carrying Ken's case. And Uncle Bob was testing its weight and saying, 'Strike me pink, boy, what have you got in it?' And Auntie Kath was telling everyone to hurry off to the bathroom and wash for tea because it was spoiling. And Joan was saying, 'Gee whiz, Ken, your case is full of tins. No wonder it was heavy.' And Auntie Kath, with a look on her face that might have been an angry look, was saying, 'I told her not to send anything. Goodness me; Helen's the limit. Your mother's really very naughty, Ken. You couldn't eat this lot if you stopped a week.' And Uncle Bob was saying, 'She means well. Off to the bathroom, kids.' And before they were out of the room Ken was sure he heard, 'It's so humiliating.' And then there was a blood-curdling scream from the cat; Francie had tripped on it.

Ken couldn't sort out what he heard any more; it merged into a continuous din. He wished with all his heart he had not come.

Chapter Three

THE BOOK

After tea, Francie said, 'Ken's going to play Tops and Tails with me.'

Joan said, 'Did you bring your stamps? I've got some swops.'

Hugh said, 'I reckon we ought to think about getting down to the tent.' (He wondered whether he would be brave enough to go if he left it until late.)

Uncle Bob said, 'I'll give the railway station a ring to see if anyone's handed in your purse.'

Auntie Kath said, 'You children run along and entertain yourselves. There's an Australian film on television, there's Scrabble or there's the book. You needn't wash up, Joan.'

Francie said, 'I'm staying up till nine o'clock tonight, aren't I?'

They went into the living-room and Hugh switched on the television. (He would be brave enough to go later; of course he would.)

Francie got her game of Tops and Tails and

spread the cards on the floor and shrieked when she matched the elephant's bottom to the milkmaid's top.

Auntie Kath yelled, 'The Scrabble's in the drawer. It'll make you think. Do you good, Hugh darling.'

Joan brought in her stamps.

Hugh yelled, 'What channel's the film on, Mum?'

Uncle Bob yelled, 'Francie, I'll tan your hide. You've been cutting up the phone book again.'

Auntie Kath yelled, 'Channel 2.'

Joan said, 'I found a three-cornered Fiume in an old picture-book Dad had when he was little. Did your mum save stamps when she was little?'

Hugh yelled, 'There's no film on. It's a bloomin' old sports show or something.'

Uncle Bob called, 'No purse handed in, lad. We'll fix you up, don't worry.'

Francie nagged, 'Tops and Tails, Ken. Tops and Tails, Ken.'

Auntie Kath yelled, 'You must have the wrong channel.'

Ken, dazed, thought he was swaying from one side of the room to the other, thought he was being cut up in slices: one slice for Francie, one for Hugh, one for Joan, one for the television, one for his Auntie and Uncle, but none for himself. 'I reckon . . .' he said. But no one heard.

Uncle Bob walked through on his way to another

room. 'Enjoying yourselves? That's the spirit. Hugh, show Ken the book. I'm sure he'd like to see it.'

'Aw,' said Hugh, 'I want to watch the film. You show him, Joan.'

'Blow the book. We're looking for stamps, aren't we, Ken?'

'Tops and Tails,' shrieked Francie.

Auntie Kath yelled, 'Sorry, Hugh darling. The film's not on until half past eight and it's not the one I thought it was. The Australian film was last week. You wouldn't like this week's a bit. All hugging and kissing. There are some toffees in the letter-rack, if you want them.'

Joan said, 'That reminds me. Where's the chocolate, Hugh?'

Uncle Bob walked through again on his way back to the kitchen. 'Here are some peanuts, kids.'

'Peanuts,' shrieked Francie, 'peanuts, peanuts!'

'Did you really bring any swops, Ken?' asked Joan.

Hugh flopped down with a battered book in his hand.

'Have a look at this, Ken. It's an old picture-book Dad had as a kid. Only found it last week. Published in 1895. Imagine that. Dad wasn't alive then, of course. His grandpa gave it to him. *He'd* had it when he was a kid. Now it's mine.'

'It's *ours*,' said Joan.

'Mine, too,' shrieked Francie.

'There's a beaut story in it about two murders on the Desmond Creek. It's all true, you know. With a drawing and everything. Fancy Dad reading about it when he was a kid and not knowing.'

'Ken doesn't know what you're talking about, Hugh.'

'Of course he does. You know, Ken: the Desmond. The creek down at the bottom of the hill. Our creek. The spring. The one we've got the dam on. Yeh, of course you know; I knew you did. Imagine Dad reading about it when he was a kid and not knowing that one day he'd buy a house and have the Desmond at the bottom of his very own hill. Well, two Chinamen were digging for gold, see. They had a shaft beside the creek. Sixty feet deep it was – the shaft, not the creek.'

'Show him the picture, Hugh,' Joan said.

Uncle Bob walked in. 'Looking at the book, eh? Imagine there being a piece in it about our very own creek. There were Chinamen here in those days, hundreds of them through the hills, digging for gold. They had a sixty-foot shaft beside the creek.'

'Ken knows, Dad. I told him.'

'It wouldn't have been on our bit of creek, of course. Ours is only a bit of a spring. Probably farther down where it's wider and joins the Woori. But interesting, isn't it? Murder and so on. Show him the picture, Hugh; it's very well drawn. It doesn't look the same now, of course. Probably didn't look the same then, either. He probably drew it from imagination. It wasn't easy to get up here from Melbourne in those days; no roads or anything, and some pretty tough characters about. Gold brings out the worst in men. They tell me diggers turned that creek over and over, three times, panning it for gold. Overgrown with blackberries now. I'll never forget when we put the dam in; talk about blackberries! Here you, young Francie; easy on those peanuts. There are other people in the house. Have some peanuts, Ken. It seems these Chinamen must have been robbed. They found one with a knife in his back—'

'That's the dishes done,' Auntie Kath said, coming in from the kitchen. 'You're on to the book, I see. Exciting, isn't it? Imagine its lying around the house all these years in your Uncle Bob's studio. Have you heard about the shaft the Chinamen had down by the creek? Sixty feet drop. And the murders? One with a knife in his back; the other at the bottom of the shaft. Did he fall or was he pushed? Show Ken the picture, Hugh. The way I look at it, one stabbed the other out of greed for gold and with his dying gasp the victim pushed the killer over the edge to his death.'

'Rubbish,' said Uncle Bob; 'the story doesn't suggest that at all. I'm convinced it was an outside job. Anyhow, Ken, you read it for yourself. What about a game of Scrabble, kids? You for a game of Scrabble with the kids, Kath?'

'That's not fair,' protested Joan. 'Dad always wins. He knows too many words.'

'Tops and Tails,' shrieked Francie. 'Tops and Tails.'

'All right,' said Uncle Bob. 'Let's have Tops and Tails.'

'Goodie, goodie,' shrieked Francie, who did get her way every now and then.

It must have been ten o'clock before Hugh set off through the garden, leading the way with the torch; not that he needed it, the moon was full and bright enough to see by, but a torch-beam was a fascinating plaything. Ken plodded beside his cousin so dog-tired that he could scarcely push one foot in front of the other. He had never had a night like it, never. His head felt sore from noise and excitement and chatter. He felt sick, but not in the usual way, not sick sick, but light-headed sick.

'No horse play, Hugh,' Auntie Kath shouted from the house. 'Remember now.'

'Yes, Mum,' bellowed Hugh.

'See you in the morning at seven o'clock,' yelled Joan. 'Did you say you had your swimming togs, Ken?'

'No,' wailed Ken.

'I'll bring some for you.'

Ken plodded on, his misery plumbing new depths.

'Goodnight, boys,' Uncle Bob called. 'If you get frightened just ring the bell. You know what I mean.'

'Chaw,' snorted Hugh.

'What bell?' said Ken, muttering deep inside against his uncle for being so stupid, for actually allowing them out of the house like this in the middle of the night. Ken hardly dared to imagine what his mother would think.

'*The* bell,' said Hugh (which told Ken nothing). '*Frightened* of what, anyway? Being frightened in the gully is silly. There's nothing down there that'd hurt a fly. You're not frightened, are you, Ken?'

'No ...' Ken wasn't sure what all this business about the gully meant. He wasn't even sure that he had heard mention of it before.

'Anybody'd think it was Africa or something. Anybody would think there were lions and tigers or something. Grown-ups give me a pain. It's a beaut tent, Ken. An *army* tent. Dad got it at Disposals. Wait till you see it.'

Hugh flashed the torch downhill but the tent was still below the dip, beyond the beam. 'We've got sleeping-bags and all. We've got a camp stove and a billy and a brush on the pole.'

'A brush?' queried Ken, stumbling unhappily to keep up, aware of the trees beginning to close in like tall buildings on either side, and of the deep silence

that lay beyond the sound of Hugh's untiring
voice.

'Yeh. A fox's tail. You know, like the big kids put
on the wireless aerials of their cars. Except that ours
is a real one. Charlie Baird gave it to me. He shot it.
Charlie Baird's always shooting foxes.'

'With a *gun*?'

'My dad's going to buy me a gun like Charlie
Baird's when I'm twelve or thirteen. There's the
tent, see. It's a beauty, isn't it? Careful here; it's
steep. If you slip you won't stop rolling till you're in
the dam. Mr Gore slipped one day when it was wet.
Whop! Talk about laugh. He went straight in. I
reckon they must have heard his yell back in
Monbulk.'

'Mr Gore?'

'Yeh. The inspector from the Water Com-
mission. It fixed him good and proper. He hasn't
been back since. Dad killed himself laughing; Mr
Gore didn't, though. It's a beaut tent, isn't it?'
Hugh stopped and proudly shone the torch all over
it.

'It's got rips in it.'

'Gee,' said Hugh, 'you'd have rips in you, too, if
you were as old as it is. Dad says there's no guessing
where it's been. Up Darwin, maybe, or in New
Guinea or in Egypt. He says men who won the VC
might have slept in it.'

'It's on a bit of a slope, isn't it? We won't roll out
of it into the dam or anything?'

'Don't be silly,' said Hugh. 'Are you scared or something?'

'Of course I'm not scared.'

'Mum's never let me sleep out before. Gee, I had to talk hard. I've been bashin' her for weeks. Havin' you for company fixed it. She always gives in in the end though, if you keep at her. Is your mum like that? Mine is. Have you ever slept in a sleeping-bag? Charlie Baird says it's terrific. We're not allowed to have a hurricane lamp in case we knock it over.'

Ken's head was spinning.

'That's your bag,' Hugh said. 'That one. You've got the rubber pillow. Mum says the guest must always have the best. What colour are your pyjamas? Mine have hot stripes, red and white. I'm going to leave my underwear on in case it gets cold. Are you allowed to leave your underwear on when it's cold? I'm not. I'm going to say my prayers when I get inside the bag. You can't kneel down beside a sleeping-bag. I put my head on the bed when I kneel down. If I put me head on the sleeping-bag I'll get a crick in me neck.'

But Hugh didn't tell Ken what he prayed about. To God, Hugh said, 'Don't let me get scared, whatever you do. It'd be awful if I chickened out in the middle of the night. Charlie Baird said I wouldn't be brave enough. But I will be brave enough.'

Chapter Four

THE FOX

Ken was so terribly tired that he couldn't sleep. He would never go to sleep ever again. He ached all over. The sleeping-bag was as hot as an oven. The ground was hard and sloping and he did not like rubber pillows. His head flopped from side to side as though it had a loose hinge. He hated rubber pillows. He hated sleeping-bags. He hated tents.

There were noises. When Hugh's chatter had finally stilled, the silence Ken had longed for was not silence at all. He heard water running, an odd sound, eternal, unending, like glass crinkling or thousands of little diamonds rushing round inside a box; he heard breezes in the leaves as though the pages of books were turning; he heard whispers like distant conversations, like trees talking to each other; he heard insects humming and drumming; he heard the earth stirring and the sky sighing. He heard the world turning round, creaking like an old wheel. It was awful.

He heard Hugh breathing steadily, regularly, in

and out. He heard Hugh sleeping. Hugh was lucky. It wasn't fair. Hugh could sleep, but Ken couldn't. But Hugh wasn't asleep, not really. He was simply trying to make it sound as though he was.

Ken could see the tent, moonlight like a coat of paint on the outside, a prism of gloom on the inside; shadows; vague shapes that might have been there or might not have been there.

He sensed the presence of things that he knew he could not see; he built them up out of nothing into solid objects that he could almost feel in his hands: the tail of the fox on the pole, the torch near Hugh's head, the handbell beside the camp stove, the black billycan that they would boil water in to make tea when morning came. They were real things, everyday things, ordinary things. Except the tail of the fox; all except that. They vanished after a time.

He heard the water, tinkling like diamonds, running on and on and on, never stopping, over the spillway of the dam. Then he could see it with his eyes shut, and the tighter he shut his eyes the clearer it became; water twinkling and tinkling, over the concrete lip of the dam, down into the mud, down into the jet blackness of tree roots and soil and humus, under the earth, inside the earth, still twinkling and tinkling, still running on.

Then there was light, a glowing, yellow light. He had seen light like it before, in the forest, in the bus, but this time it was different; it came from hundreds of golden globes. And trees grew up out of the earth into the light, and ferns as tall as houses nodding on sleepy stems, vines with flowers on them, canes growing as he watched them, long canes with huge thorns. And still the water twinkling and tinkling, running on into the golden glow, now into pools and ponds that reflected the trees and the ferns and the vines and the sky. There was only one colour: everything was gold. But when Ken looked at his hands to see if they were of gold also, his hands were not there. He had lost them. No hands, no arms, no legs, no body. Nothing.

Two golden men sat beside a hole in the shining ground eating golden sweet corn dripping with golden butter. Ken asked them if they had seen him anywhere because he was lost, but because he was lost and wasn't there they didn't hear him. They were arguing about something, but Ken couldn't understand what they were saying. It was a very peculiar language.

There were birds in the golden forest, golden parrots screeching, 'Tops and Tails. Tops and Tails,' and golden finches and golden robins incessantly chattering. There was a golden motor-car, upside-down, its wheels still spinning. Golden purses brimming with golden coins hung like golden fruits from the golden boughs. Golden petals dropped from flowers; golden leaves fluttered from trees and the golden men argued.

Ken began to understand the language; he had

never heard it spoken before but he began to understand it. They were arguing about the hole. It was
sixty feet deep. One man wanted to make it deeper.
'Sixty-four feet,' he said, 'that's where we'll find the
peanuts. Then we can give them to Auntie Kath.
She's so short of peanuts.'

'Rubbish,' said the other man. 'I know more
words than you do and I want to play Scrabble. I'm
sick of digging for peanuts.'

The argument became heated and Ken felt very
angry. He knew perfectly well they would find the
peanuts a further four feet down because he could
see them clearly. Some of the peanuts were in
shells; others were already salted, in packets. 'Get
the peanuts,' he yelled at them, 'don't waste time
arguing.' But because he was lost and wasn't there
they didn't hear him.

'You stupid people,' he yelled at them. 'You've
left all the lights burning, you're stuffing yourselves
with sweet corn, your car's broken down, and the
peanuts are there in the ground all the time waiting
for you. I can see them. They're there. All you've
got to do is dig four more feet.'

But the second man leapt to his feet with a knife
in his hand and drove it deeply into the other man's
chest. 'If you won't play Scrabble with me,' he said,
'I'll find someone who will.' Then he slipped on the
shining golden ground and fell shrieking into the
pit.

Hugh was shouting. 'It's only the screech-owl. It

can't hurt you, Ken; it can't hurt you. Only the screech-owl.'

Ken was trembling all over, wet with perspiration, so hot he could scarcely breathe. He was struggling inside his sleeping-bag, struggling to sit up, and Hugh's hands came out of the gloom towards him. Ken shrank from them, fearing the knife.

'Fair go, Ken. Snap out of it. Only the screech-owl. Only a bird.'

'A bird?'

'Gee whiz; I thought you were sick or something. Talk about a performance.'

Ken was all right again, awake again, panting for breath.

'Will I take you back to the house? I don't want you sick down here.'

'It's just that I'm so hot,' Ken said. 'It's the sleeping-bag.'

'You don't want to go back to the house?'

Of course he did. He wanted to go back to the house more than anything else in the world. (So did Hugh.) But Ken couldn't say so. He couldn't admit that to Hugh. 'I'm all right,' he said, 'just a dream ... just the screech-owl ...'

'Are you sure?'

It was strange the way Hugh sounded. It sounded as though he was accusing Ken of something, as though Hugh might have guessed that he was terrified and was calling him a cry-baby. But it was not that way at all. Hugh was shaking like a jelly.

'I'm all right,' Ken said, and wriggled back into his sleeping-bag and settled his head on the horrible wobbly pillow. 'It'll be beaut in the morning, won't it,' Ken said, 'having our breakfast and the swim and all?'

'Yeh.' Hugh crawled back to his bag, puzzled and wildly uneasy, but soon everything was quiet again, except for the whispers and the rustlings and the creakings and the water tinkling like diamonds in a box.

There was a sort of half light that didn't really tell a boy what time it was. It might have been five o'clock; it might have been six o'clock. Ken didn't know what time the sun usually got up in the morning, anyway.

It was not so easy to hear the water now, because the forest was waking up. There was the beat of the wings – magpies or kookaburras or crows – something big. There was the chatter of little birds – like small children in a schoolyard – spreading into deep recesses of the bush; the crowing of cockerels in the distance and a squawking disturbance in a fowl yard; the sound of a motor-truck labouring up a hill a long way off; a rhythmic beat somewhere downstream, a pump of some kind, that put a throb into the ground like a very slow heartbeat.

Ken had had enough of the sleeping-bag, of all

its aches and heat and mosquito bites, of all its weary hours of listening to sounds. He had longed for the light, and now it had come. Everything had been black, absolutely black after the moon had set, and then he had opened his eyes and found the half light. It was wonderful.

He squirmed out of the bag like a caterpillar shedding an old skin and sat for a while with his numbed head in his hands. He needed a long, long drink of water, but he knew he was not supposed to drink water out of dams or creeks unless it was boiled first. At the moment that swim of Joan's didn't seem to be a bad idea at all. Perhaps the water wouldn't be cold after such a night.

Outside it was neither warm nor cold, dark nor light, and the water in the dam looked like fat that his mother had poured into a bowl to cool: cloudy, greasy and grey. The trees looked enormous, like giants on tip-toe peering down at him, looked as though they belonged more to the sky than the earth. The sky was leaden and mysterious, with a bit of night in it and a bit of silver in it. And at the very bottom of everything was Ken beside that un-inviting bowl of soft fat, feeling like a speck of life under a microscope, beneath those enormous trees and tremendous sky.

He stretched himself nervously, wanting to yawn, wanting to scratch, wanting to murmur, but not brave enough yet to make a sound. Everything was so very different from what he was used to, and not an hour away by car was his own home, standing darkened, quiet and empty in that orderly suburban street. Blinds drawn, doors locked, gates bolted. No one was at home at his house. They had gone to Mildura for a weekend golf tournament, hundreds of miles away. 'Good for business,' his mother had said to his father. 'We really must go, dear. *Everyone* will be there.' So they had gone. They had dropped Ken at the railway station and had gone.

He stood on the floor of the forest, drooping, lost, and desperately lonely. Hugh was only a couple of paces away, so close, and all the others were up there in bed just over the brow of the hill, close enough to run to in a minute or two, but they were not his sort of people; he had always thought they were, but they weren't. They were strangers who lived by different rules and to different standards. Too noisy; all too child-like – if that was the word? It was one of his mother's words, after all. Or too happy. They made him nervous with almost everything they did. They spoke differently, thought differently, behaved differently; even the food on their table was different. And they belonged to this strange, strange place that screeched in the night and turned to gold in dreams. He had so hoped that everything would be all right in the morning, but it wasn't.

He could see the big birds now: big, heavy birds with thudding wings passing like spirits between the tree-trunks and the boughs. He saw a rabbit; one, two, five rabbits that darted like quicksilver the instant his eyes met theirs. They leapt and his heart leapt with them.

Then he saw a dog, or sensed it perhaps. It was gliding, not really running or trotting or loping. It passed across the open brow of the hill, across that narrow clearing between the two masses of forest, a clearing like a city street brooding at the foot of skyscrapers. The dog grew out of the gloom, became almost solid, almost real for a few seconds, then dissolved against the gloom again, against the scrub and tangled grass at the fringe of the forest clearing. It had moved like liquid, like oil. Something about it quickened his heart again; something about it drew his eyes into the gloom and sent them racing along the forest fringe like feelers, trying to fasten on to it again.

He found it, a lithe, long and supple shadow gliding silently through the gloom. He had never seen a living fox before, but that was what it was. In the moment of recognition even the colours made sense. He decided that it was red, that it was very beautiful, and that it carried a gaudy bird in its mouth.

'Fox,' he screamed, 'fox, fox, fox! It's got Joan's bantam.'

The fox jumped as if glanced by a bullet and streaked into the bush, into the dense undergrowth of dogwood and blackberries and acacia and ferns that plunged steeply towards the creek-gully

downstream from the dam, and Ken responding to an impulse that he didn't wait to question went after it.

'Stop, fox,' he screamed. 'Stop, fox. Stop. Stop. You can't have Joan's bantam.'

He ran, for the moment not knowing that his feet were bare, that he wore only his pyjamas, that the bush was sharp and rough and thick and waking to a frenzy. Little birds scattered. A cloud of startled starlings rose up, showering leaves and tiny dry twigs. Rabbits bounced like brown balls. Hugh, from somewhere, wailed faintly, 'Wassup? Wassamatter?' Ken yelled, 'Stop, fox.'

But the fox took a path well beaten down by the feet of animals, and melted into the shadow. Ken took the path, too, the very same path, until it narrowed in height and width and became a tunnel in the vegetation that only a fox or a cat or a thin boy on his hands and knees could push through. Ken got that far before he stopped to think. He was calling to the fox, 'Come back. Please bring back Joan's bantam,' when he first started feeling the pain. There was blood on his cheek from a deep scratch, blood on his legs from more scratches, blood on his hands and arms, thorns in his feet, tears in his pyjamas.

Ken couldn't believe it.

'Golly,' he whimpered, and heard the bell ringing. Clang. Clang. Heard Hugh yelling, 'Fox! Fox!'

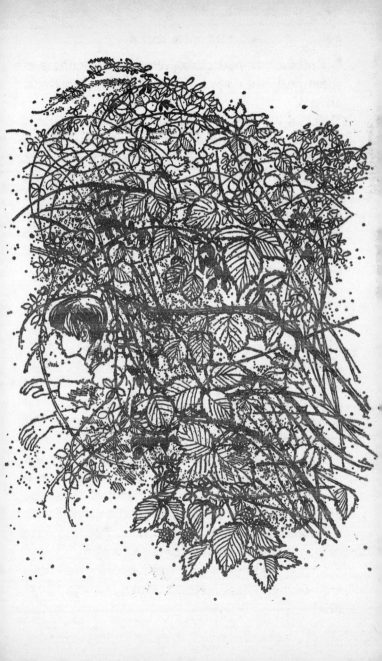

But the fox had gone. There were feathers in the tunnel, but no fox. Ken was in the tunnel, too, snared.

When he tried to back out, he couldn't. Blackberries stopped him. The stems were an inch thick; the thorns were like the claws of wildcats. They had allowed him in, but they would not allow him out. When he had not known they were there, they had not stopped him. Now he could see them, now he could feel them, now they pricked at him every tiny backward move he made. Now they stopped him because he knew they were there.

'Golly . . .'

Hugh started calling in an oddly strained and distant voice, 'Ken. Ken. Ken.'

'I'm here.'

'Where?'

'In the blackberries. I'm caught.'

'What blackberries? Where are you caught?'

'Over here. I can't get out. I can't move. I'm tangled up in thorns.'

'Yeh, but *where*? I can't see you.' Hugh's voice hadn't come any closer and sounded almost frightened. Ken was sensitive to that sort of thing; he always knew when people were nervous.

'I don't know where. Over here. You can hear me, can't you? You must know where I am.'

Hugh didn't say anything. Hugh didn't answer.

'Hugh!'

'Yeh.' But the reply came after another pause.

'Come and help me. Help me get out.'

There was that same sort of pause again; that same, strange, sagging silence.

'Hugh,' Ken called. '*Help me.*'

Hugh must have had the bell still in his hands. He started ringing it again, hard. And while he rang it he didn't shout to Ken, didn't call back, just rang and rang the bell.

The bell stopped.

'Hugh,' Ken yelled, 'why won't you come and help me?'

'I can't.'

'Why can't you?'

'I can't. I can't.'

'*Why?*'

Hugh suddenly cried out. 'You shouldn't have gone there. Not in the gully. You shouldn't, you shouldn't. No one ever goes there.'

'Why?' wailed Ken.

'Even the horses won't. They shy away. Even the dogs won't. I don't know why, but no one ever goes there. Gee, Ken . . .'

Chapter Five

THE HOLE

Uncle Bob came bounding down the hill half dressed, one slipper on, one slipper lost, holding up his trousers with one hand, brandishing a hoe in the other, yelling, 'What is it, son?' Behind came Auntie Kath in her nightgown, but Joan stopped on the brow of the hill beside a trail of feathers. No one waited to hear her, but she was sobbing, 'Samson's dead. I didn't lock him up. I forgot to shut the chookhouse door.' Francie wasn't there, neither in sight nor coming. Francie would have slept through an earthquake.

'For heaven's sake,' Uncle Bob yelled. 'Is it a snake? What is it?'

Hugh floundered uphill towards his father, with the clapper of the bell striking oddly. 'Dad, Dad ...'

The man reached the boy. 'Snake?'

'No, no, no.'

Uncle Bob was short of breath, pale, and shaking. 'What's the bell for? What's the fuss?'

'Ken's in the *gully*. He's caught. He went after the fox.'

'What fox?'

'The fox with the bantam.'

Auntie Kath arrived, panting out her questions, the same questions all over again, and Uncle Bob raised his voice over her, 'It's all right! Only a fox. It's got one of Joan's bantams.'

'Oh dear,' sighed Auntie Kath. She knew that that was far from all right.

'But, Ken,' cried Hugh. 'He went after it and he's caught in the blackberries down in the gully. You know, the gully, the awful part.'

'Soon get him out of there,' Uncle Bob said. 'How's he caught?'

'I don't know.'

'Really, Hugh.' Uncle Bob started off across the hill, irritably, then shouted back, 'I've lost a slipper. Find it for me.'

Auntie Kath ruffled her son's hair. 'Find it for him, Hugh. He's upset. He thought it was a snake.'

'It's worse than a snake.' Hugh mumbled; 'it's the gully.'

'That's being silly. Now run along. Find your father's slipper.'

'But the *gully*, Mum.'

'Hugh,' she said sharply. 'Enough of that. The gully is no different from anywhere else. Run along. Do as you're told.'

Joan came wandering down, sobbing to herself. 'Poor Samson. I've failed him. I didn't shut the door. With Ken coming an' all, I forgot to shut the door. It's my fault; I've killed my Samson.' Then she thought of Samson's two wives, Delilah and Jezebel, and wailed and headed back up the hill again as fast as she could run. 'Please, please, please,' she cried. 'Please, God.'

Auntie Kath had started hurrying towards her to comfort her, but was left standing, still with her arms outstretched. 'Oh dear,' she sighed, remembering the tragedies of her own girlhood, 'thank heaven I'm not a child any longer ...'

Ken remained crouched in the tunnel, that track that animals had made through the blackberry thickets. He was afraid to move, almost afraid to breathe, because with the tiniest movement the thorns dug into him like teeth. It was like being caught in the jaws of something. Then Uncle Bob called, 'Where are you, Ken?'

'Here.'

'That's not helping me, boy. I can't even see you.'

'I'm here,' he whimpered, 'in here. I don't know exactly where. How'd I get here? It's awful.'

'If you don't know how you got there, Ken, I'm sure I don't know.' Then Uncle Bob drew a sharp breath. 'Great Caesar's Ghost! What are you doing in there?'

Ken cried a little.

'Honest to goodness, boy. You *couldn't* be in there.'

'I am, Uncle Bob.'

Uncle Bob threw his hoe fiercely at the ground, tucked his shirt into his trousers with unnecessary force and buckled his belt with a wrench of his hand. Then he leant against a tree-trunk, plucked a couple of thorns from his bare foot, muttered under his breath, and with lips pursed started breathing very heavily through his nostrils. Auntie Kath recognized the symptoms as soon as she arrived: her husband was in a bad mood. It happened sometimes in the morning.

'Where is he?' she said.

'In there. Stupid little idiot.'

'Don't be hard, Bob.'

He scowled. 'I've seen some kids in some pickles in my time, but this is the limit. Take a look in there. It's ridiculous.'

'He hasn't gone in along the animal track?'

'He has, he has.'

Auntie Kath peered in but couldn't see him. 'Where?' Then, just as Uncle Bob had done before her, she glimpsed the soles of Ken's feet – Ken in his pyjamas, in a huddle, possibly seven or eight yards into the thicket. That thicket that filled the gully and straddled the creek for hundreds of yards downstream, that mass of blackberries and scrub and ferns fully ten to fifteen feet high out of which rose the gnarled and enormous blackwoods and the column-like trunks of towering eucalypts. 'Bob,' she breathed, shocked. 'What are we going to do?'

'It's a good question,' he said.

'We've got to get him out somehow.'

He snapped at her. 'That's something I don't need to be told.' Then he was sorry and squeezed her hand. 'We'll think of something.'

'Quiet,' she whispered, 'he'll hear you. It'll frighten him.'

'We'll have to cut him out, I suppose, bit by bit, cane by cane. It'll take hours. It'll take all day ... The things that happen to us.'

Ken called in a trembling little voice. 'Why can't you get me out, Uncle Bob?'

'We'll get you out. Don't worry about that.'

'I want you to get me out now.'

'You'll have to be patient, Ken. You can see the fix that you're in. We'll have to cut a way in. It's going to take time.'

'I want to get out now.'

'Listen, Ken,' Auntie Kath said, 'we can't reach you just yet. If someone crawls in after you, they're going to get stuck too. It'll have to be done properly. We've got to make the hole bigger and the only way we can do that is by cutting through the blackberry canes one by one and very carefully moving the pieces. If we start pulling on them or if we go at it too hard, we could hurt you. We'll drag the canes down on to you if we do that. We want you to be very brave and very calm. We want you to stay quite still. You'll not get hurt if you crouch and wait. Do you understand?'

Ken didn't answer.

Auntie Kath called again. 'You do understand, Ken, don't you?'

He whimpered a little. 'I've got things sticking in my knees and everything. There are ants and things. I want to get out now.'

'Stay with him,' Uncle Bob hissed, 'keep talking to him. Keep him calm. If he loses his head he'll tear himself to pieces. I'll get some tools; I'll be as quick as I can. Where's that Hugh with my slipper?'

Hugh was there, waiting out in the middle of the clearing.

'Have you got my slipper?' Uncle Bob called.

'Yes, Dad.'

'Well, bring it here. How do you expect me to put it on if you don't bring it to me?'

Hugh hung back because he was afraid.

'Don't force him,' Auntie Kath said quietly. 'We've got enough trouble already. Go to him, Bob, please. You know the children don't like this gully.'

So Uncle Bob went, but barked at Hugh when he reached him. 'Are you a boy or a baby? Get down there at once. You nagged your mother half silly to sleep here. And she warned you, she warned you. I don't know what you wanted to prove, but you wanted to sleep here, so now you pay the price. What *did* you want to prove?'

Hugh sniffled and felt all mixed up. He hadn't wanted to prove anything; he had only wanted to sleep in the tent. But that wasn't the truth; it was silly to lie to himself. He had wanted to prove that he was brave, to impress Charlie Baird. He had wanted to sleep there knowing that the gully was so close. He had wanted to feel the danger of it pulsing through him in the middle of the night. He hung his head.

'Well, whether you like it or not, young man,' his father said, 'you'll be spending the rest of this day in that gully. And I mean *in* it. Your precious cousin's got himself stuck. We can't push him through, we can't drag him back. I don't know what we're going to do with him. He might be stuck there for days.'

Uncle Bob pulled on his slipper and started off up the hill. He looked back, but Hugh hadn't moved.

'Hugh,' he bellowed.

Hugh shrank from that sort of anger; he wasn't used to it; he didn't like it. 'Yes, Dad,' he said. 'I'm going.' And with fright he started crying inside where his father couldn't see the tears, and started edging across the clearing, for the first time ever. He didn't know why the gully frightened him, or why it frightened horses or dogs. Only wild things lived in it. Children, and the animals that were the friends of children, feared it. It did things to fathers, too.

Even in the brightest of sunshine it had shadows in it; the sort of shadows that settled round a child's heart, that made him pause and listen and look behind. The shadows sent out signals: Beware! Yet it was all right near the dam and always had been, even before the bulldozer had torn up the under-growth and cleared the channel and scooped out the hollow beside the creek that now brimmed with water. The shadows had never started there; they began about a hundred yards downstream. But grown-up people couldn't see them. 'Rubbish,' they said, 'stuff and nonsense.' The grown-up people forgot what it was like to be a boy or girl. Charlie Baird said that even when his father had been little the local children called it the Fox Hole and any boy who braved it was a hero. It wasn't called the Fox Hole because foxes lived there, not particularly that, it was called the Fox Hole because . . . because . . . Well, no one knew, really.

Ants were crawling over Ken and making him shudder. He called to Auntie Kath to make sure she was still there.

'I'm here, Ken. Don't worry. Everything's all right.'

Then he asked her the question that was worry-ing him more than anything else, more than the discomfort, more than the ants, more than the thorns pricking at him. 'Why is Hugh frightened?'

'He's not frightened, dear, except for you. Because you're stuck. Because blackberry scratches can hurt so much.'

That wasn't what Ken meant at all. 'I mean, why won't he come over here?'

'He's doing things for Uncle Bob. Getting ready to help to cut you out.'

'But he wouldn't come when I called him, even before Uncle Bob got here.' Ken was awfully near to crying again. 'I heard you talking. I know there's something terrible here, isn't there? I'm in a trap or something.'

'No, Ken, no. Nothing like that. Do you think for one minute that I would have allowed you to sleep down here if there was anything that I knew to be dangerous?'

'That's not what Hugh said. Everybody says things that are different.'

'Ken! You are *not* in any danger. You've got my word for it. But if you move, the blackberries will scratch you. That's all that can happen. You've been here before. You've spent lots of days with us at different times. You know nothing round here has ever harmed you before. There's nothing that can.'

But Ken didn't know that and didn't believe it. Hugh was brave and strong, much stronger than

Ken, and Hugh was frightened. It didn't matter what Auntie Kath said now; nothing could change what Hugh had said before.

'I want to get out,' he murmured, 'I don't like it in here.' But she didn't hear him. And the sun was coming up; there was that change in the light that meant that the sun was near; that gradual change from grey to gold, pale gold, washed-out gold up there among the heights above him, where leaves ended and sky began. When he twisted his head – cautiously, carefully, flinching from thorns – he could see flecks of gold appearing in the midst of that oppressive mass of leaves and twigs and thorns and vines and boughs that bore down upon him. He was trembling now and though he tried to stop it, he couldn't. The tremble was in his arms and in his legs and in his teeth.

'I'm trapped. I know I'm trapped. They'll never get me out. How did I get in here? I must have been crazy or something.'

Auntie Kath was talking to him, but he didn't listen to her. She was only saying the same old things in that quiet, rather sing-song sort of voice that women used when they spoke to very little children. She was frightened too. He could hear it in the way her voice went round and round. Talking all the time, but not saying anything. Like a lullaby. Or like the lady next door, at home, talking to her three-year-old when he had climbed that day on to the roof and sat on the ridge and everybody had thought he would fall and be killed.

'Hi.'

It was Hugh. It was Hugh's voice.

'Golly,' said Ken, immensely relieved. 'You've come.'

'Yeh. I'd have got here before, but I've been busy helping dad. Looking for tools. How you doin'?'

'Better now. Much better now.'

Ken couldn't see that Hugh was shaking or that Auntie Kath was tightly holding his hand and whispering, 'See the difference it makes having you here; that's a good boy.'

'We'll be getting you out soon,' Hugh said. 'Dad'll be here with the tools in a minute.'

'I thought you said you were helping him?'

'I was . . . I – I have . . . It's just that . . .' Hugh's voice broke – to his own dismay. He couldn't think of a thing to say because he knew that Ken suspected that he was lying. Auntie Kath suddenly started prattling about Uncle Bob going back to dress in stouter clothes, but it was too late. Nothing that anybody could say any more would calm the fear that ran wild through Ken. It was like a tongue of fire leaping through him. 'I'm in a trap,' he screamed.

They started shouting at him, yelling at him to be still. 'No, no, no,' Auntie Kath pleaded. 'Don't struggle. Lie still.'

But Ken couldn't stop himself. The panic was

overpowering. The urge to do something, to do anything, was more than he could possibly resist. He fought to get out backwards, but couldn't; he fought to go ahead, he wriggled and struggled and kicked.

'Stop it, Ken,' shouted Auntie Kath. 'You'll do yourself an injury. Stop it, stop it.'

Then the ground underneath Ken began to move, to bend, to sag. He clawed for a handhold, but the handhold moved with him. He shrieked. And lost his feet, felt them going, felt them sliding down, felt the earth breaking into pieces, cracking, crunching, splitting.

Ken shrieked and shrieked and shrieked, then suddenly was breathless and quiet, with his heart pounding against his ribs, with bright blood on his hands from new cuts, with his lips drawn back and dry.

The slide had stopped. Everything was soft, but movement had stopped. He was embedded up to his hips. A curious substance was wrapped about his legs. He could flex his toes but couldn't see them. He could hear things falling but couldn't see them either. He had dropped seven or eight feet and was caught below the level of the ground in a deep bowl of humus, in a web of roots, rubbish and sticks, in a web held by roots still anchored in the crumbling earth.

Ken looked up fearfully into a tangled rectangle of light and shade. Golden light was flowing through the sky; golden leaves and golden boughs far out of reach.

Voices and cries were coming from up there, but they didn't make sense; they were too far away and out of reach. All that made sense was his dream. The memory of it came back to him so forcefully that it dulled him to everything else, even to danger. He knew where he was. He was in the hole into which the golden man had fallen, shrieking. But it wasn't a dream any longer; it was real. And the things he could hear falling were fragments of timber and lumps of earth flaking from the sides of the shaft and dropping sixty feet to bottom.

It had to be that hole. He didn't know why; but it had to be it.

'Ken! Ken! Ken!'

The frantic call was so far away, so distant in his mind that he didn't even answer it.

He was in the golden hole where the peanuts were.

'Ken, Ken! Oh dear God. Ken!'

'Daddy, Daddy, Daddy.'

Then more cries and a man's voice, 'Oh my God, it can't be true.'

Ken wanted to answer them, in a way, but he couldn't. He didn't seem to have any breath left. Then he had an urge to escape and struggled to get his legs up. They wouldn't come.

'Is Ken dead, Daddy?' (Hugh, like a little boy, saying *Daddy*.)

There was a swishing sound, almost like a whip, and grunts and gasps and orders snapped out. 'The slasher's the quickest. Beat it down. Drag it out of the way. Get that rake on it, Kath. Rope, Hugh. Move, boy, move; I want some rope.'

Ken still struggled to bring his legs up and there was movement around him again, odd movements in the sagging cushion of humus that supported him. Ken began to understand what they meant and watched them, fascinated, horrified. Holes were appearing, fine hair roots were slowly emerging from the sides of the shaft as if they were growing out of it, or were being drawn out of it, and earth was still falling, pattering, shifting, showering, and something sharp was crawling or scratching over his feet.

Suddenly, he shrieked again. Suddenly, his voice seemed to come back. *'Uncle Bob ...'* But there wasn't any sound. Ken only thought there was.

The cushion broke into shreds and tatters and dust, a cascade of leaves and twigs and mould tearing through the breaking web of roots, and Ken dropped in the midst of it.

Chapter Six

THE CAGE

Joan was up near the top of the garden sitting on the fowl-house step cuddling her bantam hens, cooing to them, when she heard Francie talking to herself. Francie was picking dahlias. She had a bunch almost as big as herself. 'Everybody's gone away. They're all meanies going away. I'm not allowed to pick dahlias. Mummy said she'd smack me if I picked dahlias, but Mummy's gone away. I'll ask Tommy Baird to marry me. I like Tommy Baird better than Charlie Baird. Tommy Baird wouldn't go away. They're all meanies going away. Mummy's gone away. Daddy's gone away. Joan said shut up to me. Joan's not allowed to say shut up to me . . .'

Hugh came floundering across the garden from the direction of the house calling for Joan, calling her name over and over again as though his life depended upon her answer.

'Here,' she yelled. 'The chook-house. The rotten old fox didn't get Delilah or Jezebel.'

'You all went away from me,' shrieked Francie

and dropped her dahlias. 'You're all meanies, you are, going away from me.'

Hugh had a stitch and had to press his side and the sight of Francie rushing at him, all steamed up over something, made him angry. Francie, even though she was little, had no right to get steamed up over anything, not now. He raised a fist and Francie stopped in her tracks. 'You're not allowed to hit me,' she shrieked. 'I'll tell Mummy you hit me.'

Hugh still pressed his side and glared at her, unjustly accused, then panted at Joan, 'Ken's dead, I think.'

Joan's face went bloodless.

'He's disappeared. The ground swallowed him up. It did. It just swallowed him up.'

Joan couldn't say anything; she couldn't make a sound.

'Ken dead,' shrieked Francie. 'Ken dead like a flower. What's Ken dead for? I don't want Ken dead like a flower.'

'Gee,' said Hugh.

'I don't want Ken dead like a flower. People aren't dead like flowers.'

'What happened?' wailed Joan. 'How?'

'He went into the bloomin' old gully. He got caught in the blackberries, chasin' the rotten old fox. He was stuck there. It was awful. And then the ground opened up, just like the kids always said it would. Gee, Joan . . .'

Francie started crying. 'I don't want Ken dead like a flower.'

'I've got to get rope,' Hugh stammered. 'I suppose Dad'll have to go down to get him.'

'I don't want Daddy dead,' shrieked Francie. 'Not Daddy dead like a flower.'

Joan grabbed her and hugged her and couldn't stop herself from crying either and the bantams flew squawking from her lap.

Ken fell for hours with his eyes clamped desperately shut. He died and came to life again. Telephones rang and sirens wailed. He broke his back and spent months in hospital. He was unconscious and his mother and his father drove three hundred and fifty-seven miles at eighty miles an hour with a police escort to be at his bedside.

Then he wasn't falling any more. In an instant the cushion of humus had collapsed. In an instant Ken had fallen with it. In an instant, Ken and all the dust and shreds and twigs and leaf-mould were in a heap together at the bottom of the hole and he knew that the worst part of the fall was not the falling but the instant that it began and the instant that it stopped.

He was afraid to move, afraid to open his eyes. He waited, numbed, for the terrible pain of a broken arm or a broken leg or a broken neck.

The pain didn't come.

He tried to look at his body without opening his

eyes. He saw it as sometimes he saw it in the mirror: thin and straight, without a blemish. He looked at it carefully and everything was just the same as always. Nothing was broken. That was how he saw it with his eyes shut.

Then he began to feel pressures, weights and objects. Most of his body seemed to be a great big hand feeling things, things that prickled, things that were damp, things that were brittle and crackly, things that continued to fall. And the rest of him was like a great big nose that smelt things: musty things, dusty things, sour things like rubbish in the dark under a house. And he could hear things: a quiet patter, creaking sounds, rustling sounds, squelching sounds, but no voices. No sound of his aunt or uncle or cousins.

When he opened his eyes there wasn't any light. He wondered whether he had opened his eyes at all; everything was so black, so formless. Everything was a great big emptiness, a great big nothing. He opened his eyes again, forced them open wide, wider still. It was still a great big nothing. It was easier to see with his eyes shut.

Still the pain didn't come. Somehow, he thought it should have come.

His hands suddenly wanted to move, but all the prickly, damp, brittle and crackly things got in the way. He pushed them aside. They were all around him. He threw them aside. They were even against his face and in his hair. He clawed them aside.

His movements became panicky.

Then his eyes opened and there was a piece of light shaped like a torn page. Up and down and sideways hadn't meant anything for a while, but now there was an up. That was where the light was. He half expected to see faces looking down as mourners would look down into a grave, but no one was there. Just the light, way up top, criss-crossed with roots that looked like bony fingers, or a net, or the bars of a cage. How far? Sixty feet? But he didn't know how far sixty feet was when it was straight up and down. It might as well have been sixty miles. It might as well have been a cage with bars. It might as well have been a grave.

His hands were terribly sore. He must have skinned them. He wrung them together and licked them, but the taste was awful, like fungus. It was because everything was so sour and so wet. It was wet down here and beginning to feel wetter all the time.

Uncle Bob wielded the long-handled slasher like a scimitar, cutting viciously with the curved edge of the blade, beating down furiously with the back of the blade.

He detested blackberries, he hated the brutes; at any time a single scratch irritated him, several scratches would put him into a temper; and now something of his hatred and something of his temper and something of his desperate concern for

Ken pushed him on past the point of wisdom, until he was a man in a fury, a man in a rage with a flashing blade.

Auntie Kath was frightened, almost distracted, sometimes running her hand through her hair in her fear. She couldn't use the rake; she was too frightened of that swishing blade; too frightened of her husband's fury.

She was terrified he might slip or miscalculate and drive the blade into her or into himself.

His body worked like a machine, taking no notice of injuries or aching muscles unused to violent effort. He wasn't a big man, he wasn't deep-chested or thick in the arms, but he threshed his way on into the thicket foot by foot until he was hip-high amongst the bits, as though caught in barbed wire, with spiky lengths of cane pressed cruelly to his legs, with many lengths like arrows or spears hooked into the fabric of his shirt, with that huge, trembling wall of bramble standing up high in front of him.

He felt the scratches and the blisters forming and the jarring with each blow of the blade and the sweat and the blood breaking out of him in streams, but nothing stopped him. The agony was part of the anger of murdering the blackberries, part of the price he had to pay for doing a job the wrong way because it was the quick way. Auntie Kath had never seen her husband in a mood like it before. But she didn't know what was going on inside his head.

She didn't know that he was thinking of Ken's mother, of the woman who was Helen, his hard-eyed sister. Auntie Kath didn't know that already he was hearing the bitter words: 'My son. My only

child. I trust him to you for three days and you give him back to me dead. You were never any good from the day you were born.' They were not nice words to have ringing in one's head.

Nor were all the other words that fell into alarm-ing patterns: sentences only half thought flashing on and off, like red lights for danger flashing on and off.

'There's no hole. It's shaped like a grave. There can't be a hole. I'd have known there was a hole. It wasn't there before. It's there now. It's a shaft. It can't be a shaft. The Mines Department said there weren't any. I asked. It's not my fault. I did ask, particularly. Shafts are circular? Shafts are square? Shafts are rectangular? I trust him to you for three days and you give him back to me dead. It's the Chinamen's shaft. The Mines Department said there weren't any shafts. Sixty feet deep. He's dead. You were never any good from the day you were born. The Chinamen's shaft was filled in. That was the point of the story. They buried the Chinamen in the bottom of the shaft and filled it in. Gold brings out the worst in men. There wasn't any gold. Two lives for nothing. Now three lives for nothing. Three days and you give him back to me dead. It can't be the shaft. The shaft's downstream. The kids call it the Fox Hole. Why the Fox Hole? There's no hole; there never was a hole. No child has ever seen it. It's the Chinamen's shaft. They're buried at the bottom. Ken's buried at the bottom. The shaft was filled in. It can't be the shaft. I trust him to you for three days and you give him back to me dead.'

Then the red lights burst into a big red explosion and he dropped the slasher and couldn't go any farther and swayed on his feet and groaned, 'Oh

Kath, Kath, Kath. The poor little kid must be dead. She'll kill me. I was never any good from the day I was born.'

Chapter Seven

BULL AT A GATE

Hugh, Joan and Francie straggled down the hill with all the rope they could find: thin bits, thick bits, short bits, long bits. Joan brought her father's pipe, too. She saw it on the armchair next to the peanuts; she took the peanuts as well; she had gone into the house to get them for no reason that she knew of.

Hugh led the way into the gully, Joan went after him, but Francie wouldn't. She sat in the middle of the clearing and cried. Joan went back to her but Francie dragged against her and sat down. 'No,' Francie said, and cried.

Hugh found his father standing in blackberries up to his hips, something like a man standing in a creek swaying to the current. Blackberries hung over him also and on either side, something like a man in a doorway. Bits of blackberries stuck out of him all over, something like a savage speared to death for revenge. He was about halfway into the place where the ground had opened up and

swallowed Ken. He looked odd about the face. Hugh found his mother standing at the edge of the blackberries with her hair in her eyes and her hands clasped together. She looked odd about the face, too.

Then Joan came up and said, 'Is Ken really dead?'

But the grown-ups didn't seem to hear her.

Hugh said, 'Will I run for help? Will I go up to the Bairds?'

But they didn't answer Hugh either.

Uncle Bob said, 'The things that happen.' His voice was strained and high-pitched and unnatural.

Auntie Kath said, 'You've got to keep trying. You can't give up. That's not like you. He might be lying there injured.' Her voice was unnatural, too.

'He hasn't answered. He hasn't called out.'

'He might be lying there unconscious.'

Uncle Bob choked. 'Or dead.'

Hugh said, "Will I ring for the police? Will I get the doctor? Will I get help? Will I get the Bairds?"

'You've got to keep trying,' Auntie Kath said; 'it's not like you to give up.'

Joan said, 'I've got your pipe, Dad.'

Francie's sob came across the clearing. 'I don't want Ken dead like a flower.'

Auntie Kath said, 'But don't go at it like a mad

thing. You might cut your leg off, or more ground might give way. You've got to keep your feet clear so you can jump if you have to. For my sake be careful.'

'Do you want your pipe, Dad? It'll make you feel better. Mum always says you're no good until you have a pipe in the morning.'

Hugh said, 'Will I get Mr Baird? Will I try to get help?'

'You can't. Your mother's not dressed.'

'Gee, Dad, that doesn't matter.'

'It does matter. You don't understand. You're all in your pyjamas.'

Auntie Kath cried, 'We can't go and get dressed at a time like this. What's wrong with us all?'

'I don't want the place swarming with Bairds.' Uncle Bob's voice was still high-pitched. 'They're always right and I'm always wrong. We can do this for ourselves. I don't want the Bairds. I couldn't stand them near me. Helen will kill me. What am I going to say to her?'

'The police, Dad . . .'

'No,' he yelled, and slumped. 'How am I going to get out of this tangle?'

'Be sensible and stand still,' said Auntie Kath, 'and we'll try to help you. The children are here. They'll help. If you stand still, we'll get the blackberries away from you. Then you can start again. The quick way isn't the quickest. You'll have to be careful, Bob. It's easy to see where Hugh gets it from. Rushing at things like a bull at a gate.'

'What am I going to say to Helen? She'll kill me for this.'

'How can Helen blame you? Blame me, if anyone, for letting them sleep here. But not you.'

'It's the Chinamen's shaft. I'm sure of it.'

'It can't be. The Mines Department said—'

'Sixty feet deep. Maybe fifty feet of water in it. He's drowned, you know. With the Chinamen buried at the bottom. On our property. We've been living with it. It's been here, dwelling on us all the time, waiting for the first chance to get at us.'

'That's silly. I was with you when the Mines Department said—'

'It's why the place went cheap. We picked it up for a song, you know. We did. But the local kids had the score. They said it'd swallow you up. When you want the truth ask the kids. The kids were right. It's got a jinx on it, this place. Nothing's ever gone right. Be honest; admit it; it's never gone right for us, has it?'

Hugh said, 'The kids call it the Fox Hole. The kids have never said anything about Chinamen.'

Joan said, 'Get Ken out, Daddy. Don't leave him there. Please get Ken out.'

He looked round for his slasher, then renewed his attack against the trembling barrier of blackberries with the same headstrong fury as before.

The sun must have been climbing up over the

valley. It must have been higher than the trees. Ken wondered what he would see if it shone down the hole. But it would never shine down the hole, never ever. The dark wouldn't let it.

The dark lived in the hole. The hole was the place where the night came from. At nights when the sun set the dark rushed up out of the hole, whooshing and rumbling and roaring, and filled the world. Then when day came the dark rushed back into the hole again and shut the door after it. But Ken had fallen through the door and broken it. Perhaps that was why the dark was angry and growled so much.

It growled everywhere around him. He had the queerest feeling that he wasn't in the bottom of the hole at all, that there was more of it down below, that down there was a lot more dark skulking where everything was blackest, that down there the dark was so thick that it bubbled like tar in a tub.

Way, way up top were the sunlight and silence. Auntie Kath had said it wasn't a trap, but it was. Auntie Kath didn't speak the truth. Auntie Kath told lies. Hugh told lies. Joan told lies. Uncle Bob told lies, too. He'd die in the bottom of the hole with no one to talk to.

It was a dungeon with a little window with bars across it way, way up in the wall. It was like a thousand years ago when people were put in dungeons and left there for ever. They had rats to listen to, then, scuttling. They had water to listen to, dripping. And only when they shut their eyes could they see anything at all. Then they could see the dungeon as if there was a light on – sixty feet deep, full of dark and spiders and centipedes, with things falling all the time – and they opened their eyes again quickly because they couldn't stand what they saw. It was not as awful seeing only the dark; it was much more awful seeing what was really there.

'Ken. Are you there, Ken? Can you hear me, Ken? Will you answer me, Ken . . .? The poor kid must be dead. I can't see a thing. It's as black as pitch. There's water, I think. I can see water.'

Hugh and Joan dragged half-rotten logs out of the bush to help weigh down the blackberries so they could get nearer to their father, so their mother could get nearer to him, too. She was frantic; she was sure he would kill himself. 'Be careful, Bob,' she implored, 'you're too close to it. You'll fall in.'

'Dad's got to the hole,' yelled Hugh. 'He's got there. Good on you, Dad. Can you see him, Dad?'

Francie came screeching across the clearing. 'Ken's not dead like a flower. Hooray, hooray.'

'Be quiet,' Uncle Bob shouted, 'for heaven's sake be quiet, everybody. Keep that kid quiet. She's like a factory whistle . . .'

'Uncle Bob, Uncle Bob. I'm here, Uncle Bob. I can see you, Uncle Bob. Please get me out, Uncle Bob.'

'He's there. I can hear him. He's alive.'

Uncle Bob's knuckles went to his eyes and pressed hard against them. Auntie Kath might have guessed the truth about him, but the children never knew that men cried sometimes. They didn't hear the sob that choked him up, because they were cheering.

Chapter Eight

FOUR MORE FEET

Hugh's torch came down into the hole on a length of string.

'We're lowering the torch to you,' Uncle Bob called, 'then we'll pull the string up again and measure it. We want to know how deep you are.'

Uncle Bob had rolled a log across the middle of the hole and he slid the torch over it so that it came down the centre where he could wiggle it past the roots that stuck out of the walls like long, bony fingers. The torch turned slowly on the string and looked like a pale yellow eye or a pale golden globe or a flying saucer or something groping down towards the earth at dusk. Then the string snagged and the torch rocked backwards and forwards and the beam of light moved to and fro across Ken like waves running up and down a beach. It was a funny feeling watching it. When the light went over him he could feel it.

'What's happened?' Uncle Bob called.

'It's stopped coming.'

'Can you reach it?'

'I can't stand up. I'm frightened to stand up in case I sink. It's squelchy.'

'Would you be able to reach it if you could stand up?'

'I don't think so, Uncle Bob. I think it's too high.'

Uncle Bob tugged to free it and the beam of light jumped about like a crazy thing. 'No good,' he said, 'watch out below,' and tugged harder until the string broke at the tangle and the beam of light suddenly dived like something alive. It struck Ken on the shoulder and dropped only inches from his hands. It hurt, and made him more aware of a sneaking little pain in his chest that he had been trying to ignore, but the horrible flutter in his heart did seem to go away a bit and the awful shiver in his jaws that made speaking so difficult was easier. To have a light in his hands seemed to change him from a frightened little animal back into a boy again.

'I've got the torch,' he cried.

'Good lad. Wave it from side to side; it'll help us judge how deep you are. You're not as far down as we thought.'

Ken moved the torch as he had been told to do and Uncle Bob said, as though surprised, 'That's fine. It can't be much more than thirty feet.'

'But it's got to be sixty,' Ken cried.

'What's that?'

'It's sixty,' Ken cried. 'It's got to be sixty.'

'Why? Why? Whatever for?'

'It's the shaft. It's the Chinamen's shaft.'

'Good heavens, boy. What a thing to say. Of course it's not.'

'But it *is* the Chinamen's shaft. I *know*.'

Uncle Bob's head and shoulders, that Ken had been able to see, swayed out of sight. Voices dropped. Ken couldn't hear them any more.

'I know it's the shaft,' he murmured to himself. 'They know it, too. They're still telling lies.'

'Ken.'

It was Uncle Bob again.

'We're going to drop you a rope. Can you tie a reef knot?'

'What's a reef knot?'

'All right. Don't worry. I'll tie it myself. The rope will come down with a loop in it. I want you to pull the loop up over your legs, like pulling on a pair of pants, up and under your armpits. It's got to fit tightly. If it's not tight, I'll make the loop smaller. Do you understand?'

'Yes, Uncle Bob.'

'The rope will be down in a minute. In the meantime stay as still as you can.'

'Why, Uncle Bob?'

'Why what?'

'Why must I stay still?'

There was a pause and Ken didn't like it. He knew that something was wrong. Then Uncle Bob said in that sing-song sort of voice (ringing hollow in the hole) that Auntie Kath had used a while ago, 'If it's the shaft, Ken, and we don't think it is, it should be sixty feet deep. You're not sixty feet down; nothing like it. And the fact that you haven't broken your legs or anything suggests that you've landed on something soft, perhaps a plug of humus with mud or water underneath it. I don't know, boy, I can only guess; something soft, something like hay. I want you to be as still as you can be, so that whatever it is that's down below doesn't start moving. All right?'

'Yes, Uncle Bob.'

'Good boy ... Are you hungry? Would you like something to chew?'

'Yes, please, Uncle Bob.'

'We'll tie a bag of peanuts to the rope when it comes down. Look out for them.'

'Thank you, Uncle Bob.'

His head and shoulders swayed away from that torn page of daylight again, and voices dropped again, and Ken couldn't hear. (Uncle Bob said, 'I wish the kid wouldn't be so polite. It worries me. It's not natural.')

Ken moved the light-beam round his dungeon. Higher up it was a rectangle and narrow. After all, not so long ago he had imagined that people would look down into it, as into a grave. That was how narrow it was; he had seen graves on TV. But here it was like a cave; not a cave, but like one. Here it had broken away. A mass of earth, years ago, had slipped from the walls and tumbled into the depths beneath where the dark was as thick as tar in a tub.

It had been washed away by water. Ken could see that water sometimes rose much higher than the level at which he now sat so gingerly, so nervously, so startled by every pattering sound and every squelching sound. He began to think constructively. It was a dry season; Joan had said that; they were lucky to have water in the dam. Uncle Bob had said that the creek was a spring. Perhaps in wet seasons, perhaps in winter the creek was much more than a spring and the seepage in the hole turned from mud into water many feet deep. If this had been a wet season . . .

'I would have drowned. I'd be dead.'

Ken felt sick. Dead like Grandpa. Like Auntie Prue. Like Peter Carroll who fell from a bus.

'Ken. I'm letting down the rope.'

Ken shone the light into the gloom from which the earth had slipped away. It looked as though some strange, huge, underground creature, with a taste for dirt, had bitten into the side of the shaft. Ken could almost see his teeth marks, could almost follow the closing of his jaws, could almost hear the crunch as his teeth struck rock and glanced off. He had taken a bite four or five feet deep into the wall of the shaft but had blunted his teeth on rock.

'Ken. Can you reach the rope?'

The light shone on the rock, on rock washed clean by years of water. Grey sort of rock, or sandy-coloured perhaps. Ken couldn't take the light away from it.

'Ken. I'm sure the rope is long enough. It's on the bottom. Don't leave it there, boy. Your peanuts'll spoil in the wet. *Ken!*'

'Yes, Uncle Bob.'

'Can't you hear me?'

'Yes, Uncle Bob. The rope's here. It's long enough.'

'Well, put it on. Get the loop under your armpits.'

Ken was bewildered. He wanted to say something but his thoughts trailed into nothing.

'Something's wrong with that boy. He must be injured . . . What's going on down there?'

'Uncle Bob,' Ken said explosively, 'you're rich.'

'I'm *what*?'

'Rich, rich, *rich*! There's gold down here.'

'For heaven's sake, boy, the rope! Put that rope on.'

'There's gold down here. I can see it. Specks of it in the rock. Thousands and thousands of specks all gleaming. Really, Uncle Bob. Truly.'

'I don't care, boy, if the Crown Jewels are there. Will you put on that rope! At once.'

'Golly, Uncle Bob. It's the Chinamen's shaft. I dreamt about it. Four more feet. It's just like it was in the dream, only different. The gold's not on the bottom but in the side. Four more feet. They missed it when they dug down.'

'THE ROPE.'

That shout broke into a cry of alarm. Perhaps Uncle Bob slipped but somehow recovered, because there was a shower of pebbles that fell like hailstones and pieces of dirt cracking from the walls, bouncing down, and a veil of dust puffing across that torn page of light. Ken flinched, ducking his head, and it rained on him, bits of stone, bits of dirt, mouldy leaves, sticks, thorns. Then another cry. 'Ken, Ken, are you all right?'

He couldn't answer because there were thousands of grains of dirt falling like grains of sand, and dust, and a continuing rustle and patter, and that world up there in the sunlight was so far away. It was a world that he didn't want anything to do with. It rained dirt on him and when it talked it shouted and argued and lied. It took no notice of him when he told it exciting things and it didn't know anything about the nasty pain in his chest.

Then he began to cry.

Uncle Bob crouched, trembling, near the edge of the hole, yet clear from it by a foot or two. He had thought he was on his way; he had thought he was falling, but had grabbed for the stump of a severed blackberry and slashed his right hand with thorns.

Oh, he had thought he was gone and when men fell they usually broke. Men didn't bounce the way that boys bounced.

'He's still there,' he panted. 'I can hear him crying . . . My hand . . .'

Auntie Kath was pale and shaking 'What is it that's wrong down there? Crown Jewels? What are you talking about?'

Uncle Bob sighed. 'Nothing, nothing.'

'That's not true, dear.'

'Yeh, Dad. What is it, Dad?'

He shuffled back a couple of paces and breathlessly tested the safety of the ground at his feet and hugged his hand to his side, smearing his shirt with fresh blood.

'He's the most exasperating child. If only he would do as I ask, I'd have him up in no time.'

'What are you hiding from us, dear?'

There was an odd flicker in Uncle Bob's eyes, but no one knew or cared what it meant, probably not even Uncle Bob himself. 'He says he's found gold. It's absurd, of course.'

They stared at him.

'I mean, how could there be gold? Even the creek-bed's been turned over three times. Three times. No, not gold. That sort of thing couldn't happen to us. I mean, what notice can you take of an hysterical child? He's never seen gold in his life.'

But his face was changing; the fire in his eyes was

brightening. His wife didn't answer him; his children didn't answer him, not even Francie. His hands were becoming unusually restless; he had even forgotten his wounds. Then his feet became restless and he couldn't stand still. He stammered a little: 'But there's an instinct in a man, isn't there? Part of being a man. There's a feeling. Some things we know that we've never been told. Like gold. Even the word starts the blood rushing through us. Even children know it when they see it, even if they've never seen it before. The boy's right, you know. It's my instinct and his instinct. I know. He knows.' Then his tongue couldn't keep up with his thoughts and his voice slurred and became silent.

It was funny, but Joan didn't like the things that she could see happening to her father. 'Mummy,' she said, and grasped her mother's hand and when her mother glanced down she looked strange, too.

'We're rich,' Uncle Bob said, and laughed nervously. 'Us; of all people. It's there, you know. I can feel it in my bones. The kid's found gold.'

'Gee, Dad.' Hugh was muddled. Things were going on that he didn't understand. 'What about Ken, Dad? You've got to get Ken up, Dad. I'd better get the Bairds. We'll never get him up without help.'

'Ken's down the hole,' cried Francie. 'I don't like Ken down the hole.'

'I'm going to get help,' Hugh said. 'It's the Fox Hole. I don't like Ken bein' down there.'

'Stay where you are! If I didn't want the Bairds before, I want them less now. We'll get him up, all in good time. He's all right. Nothing can happen to him.'

'But, Dad . . . You said the bottom might fall out of the hole.'

'If it hasn't fallen out by now it's not going to fall out.' He had his hands on his hips and furrows in his brow and hard lines about his mouth.

'Mum!'

'Yes, Hugh.'

When she turned to him there was that same, strange look about her mouth and eyes and forehead. He couldn't say anything into the mask of that expression; his protests dried up and wouldn't take the shape of words. Nor did his mother pursue her answer. She glanced at him, but looked through him, didn't see him. She seemed unaware that Joan had pulled her hand free and was beginning to look weepy.

It was frightening; something was happening; and the children didn't like it.

Mum and Dad had gone away somewhere and left them behind. They were all together in that strewn tangle of blackberry pieces, all scratched, all torn a little, but the children and the grown-ups were strangers. The man laughed, almost furtively; the woman giggled.

'All the things,' she said, 'I've ever wanted. I can go out and buy them.'

'No more struggle,' he said, 'no more stupid little verses on stupid little Christmas cards. No more sneers from that precious sister of mine.'

'They're not stupid little Christmas cards,' cried Joan. 'They're lovely.'

They looked at each other, the man and the woman, and smiled in the strangest sort of way.

'We're rich.'

'What's rich?' shrilled Francie.

The voice from up top started beating down on Ken, again. 'Have you got that rope round you yet?'

He didn't answer. He played the torch-beam, almost tenderly, over the rock face, watching its gleam. It was beautiful.

'Listen here, young fellow; your mother's not going to be pleased when I tell her about this!'

Ken was troubled by a moment of concern, but then he said, 'It's not my fault I'm down here. It's your fault.'

'We're not talking about whose fault it is. Do you want to die? Do you want to sink into the sludge? Your luck can't hold for ever. You'll go down like a brick.'

The voice was hard and Ken glanced up in faint surprise. That couldn't be Uncle Bob, but it was the same outline as before, the same head and shoulders; but something in the words, perhaps, re-

minded Ken of his own mother. Looking up made
him wince.

'I can't put the rope on,' he said sullenly.

'Speak up. Speak up.'

'It hurts. I can't put it on.'

'You must be bigger than I thought. I'll make the
loop larger.'

'I've got a pain.'

'A what?'

'Pain. Pain.'

'You can't have. Oh no, not at this stage of the
game you can't.'

'I've got a pain in my chest. It's all bruised, because I've looked. It's all black. It's hurting more all
the time.'

The head and shoulders swayed away and stayed
away for long seconds. Perhaps thirty seconds;
perhaps a minute. Perhaps two minutes.

Time stretched longer and longer and Ken
started shivering. It was not that it was cold particularly, but it was wet, and it was silent now,
absolutely silent: no pattering, no rustling, no
squelching.

Everything, suddenly, seemed to have come to a
stop. All that connected him to the real live world
was that knotted rope of short bits and long bits,
thick bits and thin bits, that drooped from the sky to
his feet, like a telephone cable hanging broken from
a pole when everyone's telephone had gone dead.

*   *   *

'What I'm trying to get through to you kids,' Uncle Bob said tensely, 'is that we can't have anybody coming here to help us.' He glared at them, his hands on his hips as before, his brow nervily furrowed as before.

'No one,' he said, 'not even our best friends. The gold's on the creek-reserve. It's our land in a way, of course it's our land in a way, but in another way it's not. The land along the creek and for twenty-two yards on either side of it belongs to the Government. When you get down to the law of the business, that's who it belongs to. And if it belongs to the Government it belongs to the people, to everybody, to every Tom, Dick and Harry you can think of. Anybody with a miner's licence can come in here and peg a claim, and once they've pegged it, it's theirs. They can stop here for years, build roads and dams, put up houses. They can peg it out by the acre and it's theirs for about twenty years, all for a few cents. That's the law and you can't argue with the law. You know these things as well as I do. You've learnt about the miners at school. You know what they can do. They can do almost anything.'

'But, Dad . . .' wailed Hugh.

'No buts! As soon as anyone smells gold they'll be rushing here in their hundreds. They'll be pegging claims up and down the creek for miles. And have I got a mining licence? No; and it'll be the middle of next week before I can get my hands on one. It's a holiday weekend. All the government offices are shut. And once the word's out we won't be able to call our souls our own. We won't be able to call our home our own. We could lose this to anyone; we could lose it to anyone coming in here with the right sort of licence. And as soon as Francie sees a stranger, as soon as she sees anyone, she'll be blabbing about it. You can't stop a little girl her size. You can't tell a little girl her size not to talk. She just doesn't understand. We can't get the Bairds. We can't get the police. We can't get a doctor in. We can't have anybody here but ourselves. Have I made myself plain? Have I got to say it again and again and again? We're stuck here! It's a state of siege. No one leaves this place for *anything* until I get my hands on a licence!'

He was breathing heavily. His hands were shaking.

'There's a fortune down there. It's the lode they've been looking for for eighty years, a hundred years, for I don't know how long. It's why they turned this creek over and over and over. It's why they came back here in the Depression, in the Thirties, when a man would work like a slave for a loaf of bread. They always got gold-dust out of this creek; you can get it out any day you like, farther downstream, because it's been washing away from here. Why do you think they tried and tried and tried? Not for the dust; they couldn't get enough of it in a month to pay a day's wages. They were looking for the lode; they were looking for the reef; and

it's here. It might run off in any direction. It might
run for a few feet; it might run for half a mile. I
don't know. No one knows. We're sitting on top of a
fortune and I'm not going to lose it. Can't you kids
understand what it's going to mean to you? Everything you've had no chance of getting. You name it
and you can have it; anything! A house with stairs
in it. Bikes with lights on. Beds with knobs on. A
brand spanking new Mercedes. College educations.
And you talk about going for help. All the help we
need is down there underneath our feet.'

Chapter Nine

THE TORN PAGE

The rope at Ken's side jerked suddenly, alarming him, and grains of dirt showered down from up top. There was a shadow across that torn page of light, Uncle Bob awkwardly winding the other end of the rope about the log that he had rolled across the middle of the opening to the shaft. Then knotting it and tugging on it, then leaning across the hole with all his weight bearing on to the log, showering more dirt down.

'It'll hold,' he said irritably, addressing someone Ken could not see. 'For heaven's sake, woman, don't *you* start. Haven't I stood enough from the kids? Do you think I'd go down there if I couldn't climb up again. I might be stupid but I'm not that stupid ...'

The shaft amplified his voice like a speaking tube, made it hollow, made it eerie, but dust kept coming down until Ken couldn't look any more. His eyes were filling with dust.

'Well, I can't ask Hugh to do it, can I? What sort

of a man would that be, sending his son down there? Asking his son to do something that he was scared to do himself? I repeat, I can climb a rope! Do you think I'm a weakling or something . . .?'

The dust was making Ken cough and when he coughed, it hurt, and Uncle Bob's cross voice was an extra irritant, an extra worry, part of something awful that surely could not be real; part of the other side of the conversation that Ken could not hear.

'Oh, for heaven's sake, not Francie, too. Now you've started Francie off. Heaven preserve me from females! Will someone keep that child quiet. Take her away somewhere; lose her. Put a gag on her, will you! Everybody in the district will be here. All I'm doing is going down a rope and coming up again. I'll be doing it a thousand times before I'm through. How do you think anybody ever gets up and down a shaft? Flies? This is a madhouse . . .'

Ken shrank back into himself as though sheltering from a storm. The torch-beam slanted unheeded across his lap, pouring endlessly into the black sludge, wasting itself.

'I'll be all right, do you hear? My hands are all right, they're only cut. It's a fortune down there. But we'll never know for sure, will we, until I look? I'm going to see for myself. I've got to *know*.'

Dirt came down in clouds and lumps, bouncing off the walls, pattering round Ken, striking him, terrifying him, and the rope that he couldn't see,

through eyes squeezed tight against dust, twitched against him and slapped him.

'I'm all right. How many more times? Great Scott, I'm not a child. I can climb a rope. Will you get back from the edge. Will you keep away from me. If anyone falls it'll be you. Get back. And take Hugh with you. Hugh! Will you get your mother back from the edge. Will *someone* get back from the edge. You're making me nervous. Look, if I slip now I'm gone.'

'Bob, Bob, Bob; it's not worth it . . .'

The rope still twitched and slapped and dirt still fell, but the voices stopped. All Ken could hear was the ceaseless patter and the grunting of a man gradually becoming louder. But Ken didn't look up. He remained huddled, sometimes coughing against the dust, breathing dust. It filled him; it covered him.

A weight suddenly bore down into the sludge beside him; it moved, it squelched; and Uncle Bob was panting and mumbling under his breath and coughing.

'All right,' he yelled. 'I've made it.'

The weight bore deeper into the sludge and Ken, with a flood of tears, grabbed for his uncle's trouser leg and clung to it.

'Easy, easy. I don't want to fall. Let me get my balance.'

'Uncle Bob . . .' the boy sobbed.

'Let me go, Ken, please . . . Please, Ken. I

haven't got my balance. I'm sinking. Shine that torch on my feet. I've got to see.'

His feet were not there. They must have been six inches under, squelching. Ken shone the torch up. Uncle Bob's teeth were clenched together, his face was twisted, his body was swaying, his hands were locked about the rope.

'You're dazzling me! Shine it down!'

Uncle Bob's feet had sunk to eight or nine inches under and by dragging desperately on the rope he struggled to free them, struggled to draw them out like a couple of teeth.

'Sit down, Uncle Bob!'

Ken's cry was sharp and urgent but the man still swayed back and forth on the rope, across the shaft, something like a pendulum, the movement with each sway becoming wilder, becoming less controllable. Then what Ken said seemed to make sense. To Uncle Bob it came simply as a flash of understanding. It was what the boy had done; he had had the brains or the luck to spread his weight and had not sunk.

He let the rope go, not exactly in terror, but almost, and sat heavily. He was still trapped by the feet but he didn't sink any more. He just sat there, breaking out in a sweat, shaking, trying to find his breath and his voice again. Then he wrenched his legs free, but lost his slippers. He didn't even feel them go from his feet; they remained swallowed in the sludge.

'Give me the torch,' he said, and took it. 'Where's this gold?'

'There, Uncle Bob.'

Voices, all the time, were coming down from up top, Auntie Kath's voice, Hugh's. Ken heard them, but Uncle Bob didn't.

He shone the light on the rock and gasped and his left hand grabbed at Ken's knee. 'It's here,' he yelled. 'It's true. It's here. Do you hear that, Kath? It's here.' But he didn't really speak to Auntie Kath; he didn't really know what he said.

He played the light over it – the rock and the gleam – and saw it as a huge treasure-chest filled with riches into which a man could thrust his arms. He stretched towards it, had an urge to stroke it, still heard nothing of the voices that came down from up top, or of Ken either.

'How are we going to get out, Uncle Bob? It hurts, Uncle Bob. I've got a pain.'

The man glanced up, thinking, 'I'd say it was about thirty-five feet down. Just below the colour change; thirty feet of red soil, then the grey. It's a bonanza. They've had to dig thousands of feet to strike lodes like this.'

'Uncle Bob . . .'

'Have to shore up the shaft again, though. Dangerous. That's something I'll have to learn to start with. How to do it. I can't ask anybody. I'll have to get it from books or think it up. It's a tricky business, this shinning up and down ropes. A

fortune! Ten thousand? A hundred thousand?
Gold's worth a packet these days. Maybe a *million*?'

The thought was like a hit on the head or a
breath of gas, as though his thoughts, by accident,
had solved a sacred mystery, then had rushed away
from the discovery in fright. He didn't dare even
frame the word in thought again.

The voices from up top began to break through
to him; then another sound, much closer, a sob.

On an impulse that didn't mean anything he
turned the torch-light on Ken. He was huddled; he
was filthy; his eyes were like washed-out patches in
a dirty sheet.

'Chin up, lad. Nothing that a bath won't fix.'
Then he shouted, 'Are you there, Kath?'

'Of course I am.'

'Get Hugh to lower a hammer or something on a
string. Don't use that skinny stuff again; there's a
hank of strong twine in the shed where the garden
stakes are. Better still, send down a bucket. Put the
cold chisel and the hammer in the bucket and I'll
send some sample up. They'll pop your eyes clean
out of your head.'

She started arguing about something, but Uncle
Bob wasn't interested. Ken wasn't listening either.
Ken was shrinking farther and farther into himself.
He might as well not have been there at all. He
might as well have been dead. Perhaps if he had
been dead they would have taken more notice of
him. Nothing but words rang in the shaft, and

noises in his head, and Uncle Bob's peculiar muttering.

'I'm going to need machinery. I'll shift the pump over from the dam; that'll be a start. Get the shaft thoroughly dry. Then a winch to get the ore up. What do I do with the stuff then? How do I crush it? How do I refine it? Maybe the Mines Department will put me on the track. They'll come to look at it; that's a cert; then maybe the bank'll help. I'll just have to tell the bank; that's the trouble; money, money, money; I've got to have money before I can start. Haven't even got a truck or a decent car; got nothing to carry anything in. As soon as I start ordering machinery the secret'll be out. The place'll be swarming with people pegging claims up and down the creek for miles...'

The failing torch-light had wandered back on to Ken, on to that small human huddle, barefooted and in pyjamas, covered in dust and dirt and cobwebs and fragments of leaves and tearstains. The light had not wandered back for any particular reason; but it had settled on him perhaps by chance and stayed there, gradually pulling at Uncle Bob's thoughts, gradually sharpening his conscience. It was a long and very strange moment.

Quite suddenly, Uncle Bob saw Ken as a shocked, orphaned child in rags huddled in a hole while bombs fell. That was how it came to Uncle

Bob, because when he had been a very young man, a soldier, he once had found such a child at the bottom of a shell hole in Korea. At one moment that huddle was Ken, the next moment a Korean child; the next Ken again, his own nephew, his only sister's only son. In a way the two children were the same child. Uncle Bob had leapt into that shell hole for safety and had leapt out in fright. ('Did I fire the gun that made this hole, that wrecked this hut, that killed this little boy's family?') He had run to another hole and gone back later when the bombs had stopped falling. The little boy had looked at him, and screamed, and had run away. That little boy had stopped believing in the goodness of grown-up men. So had Ken. The eyes that squinted into the torch-light were the same eyes that Uncle Bob had seen those many years ago.

He took the boy's hand in shame and shuffled closer to him and put an arm round him. After a while – it seemed like hours to Uncle Bob, but wasn't – Ken blindly pushed his face against him and cried.

In a minute or two Uncle Bob called up the shaft, 'Are you there, Kath? We're losing our light down here. The torch is going out.'

'Mummy's gone.'

It was Joan, not sounding very much like Joan at all. She sounded little again, not like a big girl ten years old.

'Where's Mummy gone?'

'With Francie. To get dressed. To bring back something to eat.'

'No sign of Hugh?'

'No, Daddy. Is there something you want me to do?'

'No . . .'

'It hurts, Uncle Bob. When are we going to go up?'

The man ran an eye up that dangerous rope of short bits and long bits, of thin bits and thick bits all knotted together. 'Soon,' he said. 'Soon as I feel up to it. It'll be a hard climb. What hurts?'

'My chest. It hurts and hurts. It hurts to breathe.'

The man felt a flutter of panic and another rush of shame.

'Where exactly?'

'Here, here, my chest . . . It sort of came on. And when I looked it was all black, see; all bruised.'

Uncle Bob didn't say it out loud, but he said it inside with bitterness, 'Ribs! Broken ribs! And that does it, doesn't it? That finally wraps it up. It's a doctor for sure; it's a hospital to patch him up. He's been waiting here with broken ribs.'

'I did tell you before, Uncle Bob.'

'I know.'

'But you wouldn't listen.'

'Yes, I know. I'm sorry, lad.'

He couldn't climb that rope. He didn't dare to climb that rope. He'd kill himself; and if he tried to

carry Ken he'd kill him, too. He couldn't climb a
rope, not really; he'd never been able to climb a
rope, not properly. Going down and going up were
two very different things, and it was only gold that
had got him down.

He was thirty-five feet below ground, sitting on a
slowly saturating heap of fallen humus, sitting on
top of a bog thirty feet deep. He couldn't stand up,
he couldn't climb; the strength was not in his arms
to climb, the suppleness was not in his body. Yet he
had done this wilfully and recklessly as a headstrong child would have done it, perhaps as his own
son Hugh would have done it, if his fear of the Fox
Hole had not prevented him. But Hugh would have
done it for Ken's sake. Hugh's reason would have
been a good reason. Children were not like men.
(He could hear himself shouting at Hugh, 'Think!
Think! Think!')

'Joan,' he called, 'I want you to do a job for me. I
want you to run up to the house and tell Mummy to
ring the police. They're to bring proper ropes or
extension ladders or something like that.'

For a while he thought she hadn't heard or
hadn't understood, but then she said in a choked-up
voice, 'Are you going to tell them about it, Daddy?
Aren't we rich any more?'

'No, sweetheart; not rich any more and nothing
to tell.' Then he lied to her, and it cost him a fortune
to tell the lie. 'It's not gold. It only looks like gold.
They call it Fool's Gold. You've got some of it in

your own collection of specimens. That's all it is. I'm sorry, Joan, all the lovely things you could have had. But it's not gold, sweetheart; it's not worth anything.'

'Daddy,' she cried.

He sighed and wished he could have seen her better.

'Look, sweetheart, it's all for the good, believe me. Don't be disappointed. We won't have all those roads and buildings and ore-crushers cluttering our gully. We won't have people pegging out claims all over our lovely hills, or chopping down our trees, or spoiling everything. It's Fool's Gold, sweetheart—'

Her cry came down the shaft. 'But I'm not disappointed, Daddy. I don't care. I don't like being rich.'

Her words fell heavily, as though weights made of lead were falling on him.

'Mummy said – Mummy said—'

But Joan choked on it or mumbled it and he didn't hear her.

What had 'Mummy' said?

That she'd rather be poor, perhaps? That she'd rather live with an honest battler than a desperate, greedy millionaire? If not, the time would have come sooner or later.

When he could bring himself to look up again, Joan had gone and the torch had failed and everything was dark except for that torn page of light overhead.

Ken stirred in his arms.

'Uncle Bob . . . That was a big fib. It's not Fool's Gold at all.'

The man who held him so firmly but so carefully had nothing to say.

'I'll keep your secret, Uncle Bob. I promise. I'll never tell, not anyone, not even my mum. I like you, Uncle Bob.'

Hugh, with the bucket and hammer and cold chisel, floundered past Joan on the hill.

'He doesn't want them now,' she said, almost wailing at him.

Hugh wasn't thinking very well. 'Doesn't want what?'

'That stuff. The bucket and things. It's Fool's Gold. Only looks like gold. He wants the police instead, to get him out.'

'Gee,' Hugh said, but not immediately, only after Joan had gone on up the hill to the house, calling hoarsely for her mother long before her mother could possibly hear her.

Then Hugh dropped the bucket with a clang and ran on to the edge of the hole.

'Hey, Dad,' he yelled. 'Charlie Baird's been catching rainbow trout down the Woori. Can I get the rods out for Ken and me?'

But no voice came up to him.

'Hey, Dad! Did you hear me? Are you all right?'

'I heard you, son. I'm all right now.'

'What about the rods, Dad?'

There was a pause and a rather odd reply, 'Thanks son, for that.'

Hugh pulled a face, a very long one, a very puzzled one, and started scratching at his head, not because it itched but because he wasn't much good at thinking, at least not then.

'Hey, Dad. What about those rods?'

A Selected List of Fiction from Mammoth

While every effort is made to keep prices low, it is sometimes necessary to increase prices at short notice. Mammoth Books reserve the right to show new retail prices on covers which may differ from those previously advertised in the text or elsewhere.

The prices shown below were correct at the time of going to press.

☐	416 24580 3	**The Hostage**	Anne Holm	£1.50
☐	416 96630 6	**A Box of Nothing**	Peter Dickinson	£1.75
☐	7497 0186 2	**The Granny Project**	Anne Fine	£2.25
☐	416 52260 2	**Sarah's Nest**	Harry Gilbert	£1.50
☐	416 51110 4	**Zed**	Rosemary Harris	£1.75
☐	416 54720 6	**Changing Times**	Tim Kennemore	£1.75
☐	7497 0344 X	**The Haunting**	Margaret Mahy	£2.25
☐	7497 0130 7	**Friend or Foe**	Michael Morpurgo	£2.25
☐	416 29600 9	**War Horse**	Michael Morpurgo	£1.75
☐	7497 0051 3	**My Friend Flicka**	Mary O'Hara	£2.99
☐	7497 0228 1	**The Vandal**	Ann Schlee	£1.75
☐	416 51880 X	**Journey of a Thousand Miles**	Ian Strachan	£1.75
☐	416 95510 X	**Ned Only**	Barbara Willard	£1.75
☐	416 62280 1	**Archer's Goon**	Diana Wynne Jones	£1.75
☐	416 22940 9	**The Homeward Bounders**	Diana Wynne Jones	£1.50

All these books are available at your bookshop or newsagent, or can be ordered direct from the publisher. Just tick the titles you want and fill in the form below.

Mandarin Paperbacks, Cash Sales Department, PO Box 11, Falmouth, Cornwall TR10 9EN.

Please send cheque or postal order, no currency, for purchase price quoted and allow the following for postage and packing:

UK	55p for the first book, 22p for the second book and 14p for each additional book ordered to a maximum charge of £1.75.
BFPO and Eire	55p for the first book, 22p for the second book and 14p for each of the next seven books, thereafter 8p per book.
Overseas Customers	£1.00 for the first book plus 25p per copy for each additional book.

NAME (Block Letters) ....

ADDRESS ....

....